THE SMUGGLER RETURNS

When Daniel Locke returns to Penhaven, the Cornish village of his childhood, he is intent on revenge against the smuggling gang who betrayed him as a young lad. What he doesn't count upon is the distraction of beautiful Jane Tregarron, who has become involved with the local smugglers to save her penniless family from losing their home. Can Daniel still inflict his revenge or will his plans be muddied by love?

Books *by* Kate Allan
in the Linford Romance Library:

FATEFUL DECEPTION
THE RESTLESS HEART

KATE ALLAN

THE SMUGGLER RETURNS

Complete and Unabridged

LINFORD
Leicester

First published in Great Britain

First Linford Edition
published 2010

British Library CIP Data

Allan, Kate.
 The smuggler retuns. - -
 (Linford romance library)
 1. Smugglers- -England- -Cornwall (County)
 - -Fiction. 2. Poor families- -England- -
 Cornwall (County)- -Fiction. 3. Cornwall
 (England : County)- -Social conditions- -
 Fiction. 4. Love stories. 5. Large type books.
 I. Title II. Series
 823.9′2–dc22

 ISBN 978–1–44480–032–6

Published by
F. A. Thorpe (Publishing)
Anstey, Leicestershire

Set by Words & Graphics Ltd.
Anstey, Leicestershire
Printed and bound in Great Britain by
T. J. International Ltd., Padstow, Cornwall

This book is printed on acid-free paper

1

'Headstrong! Foolish! Selfish!' Each word shouted by her mother was like a dart being thrown across the parlour, piercing her and hurting her.

Yet still Jane fought back. She stood close to the door, resisting the urge to flee. Her voice was raised though she tried to moderate it. 'I will not marry him! You cannot force me! You cannot make me!'

'Has your good sense completely deserted you?' Mama shook her head. Jane noticed tears in her eyes and felt ashamed at her own behaviour.

It did not prevent her asking, 'But have you no thought for my happiness?'

'You will speak with your father when he returns and that will be the end of it.'

Jane's heart thudded in her chest. Her breathing was quick. Her bones felt like lead. There had been so many times when Papa had indulged her.

This would not be such a time, she knew.

She was beaten.

Her mother, stood in front of the fireplace watching her, remained silent. The only sounds were the calm crackle of the fire and the soft pad of the rain against the window panes. The rest of the house was quiet, though each of her three sisters must be somewhere indoors. Listening.

Anger welled up inside her, stoked by hurt and humiliation. And a little fear. Fear that would grow. Jane Tregarron had no wish to become the wife of John Mandrake. Not ever.

The need to get away rose up with her anger. It became all consuming. She ran out of the parlour, snatched her cloak and bonnet from the cupboard off the hall and went straight through the front door and into the rain.

Jane clutched her cloak tightly at her neck and held her felt bonnet to her head. The wind bit and tore at her, matching her anger with its own. Making it hard to tie the ribbons. She started to run. Away from the house. Towards the town and the sea.

She would not marry him. She'd been foolish even to consider that she could be mistress of John Mandrake's household. Do her wifely duties as Mama had called it. Keep his bed warm . . . She shuddered as she glanced forward towards the harbour.

The front doors of the whitewashed stone cottages that faced the sea were barred shut. The criss-cross of streets surrounding the crescent-shaped harbour were empty. At the high point of the town the Mandrakes' grand house stood proud yet apart from it. Like a magnificent jewel in a royal crown yet haughty and forbidding. The only house in Penhaven to have a separate entrance for tradesmen.

She would never be mistress of that terrible place. Never. Not while she still breathed. Not while she still had spirit left in her to fight it. The picture could not be as black as Mama had painted. She did not believe it. Mama simply wanted her married and thought the Mandrakes a good family. When she saw her father, she would ask him for the truth.

Penhaven Cove's sweep of pale beach billowed with sand. Waves pushed up to and raced over the stone walls and jetty. The coasters and fishing vessels bobbed up and down. Dark waves chopped at their hulls, smashing themselves into white spray. The wind swept in over the sea from France and the ocean beyond. Yet the boats clung to their anchors and moorings.

Folks might do well to stick to what they know, as their housekeeper, Mrs Beresford, was wont to say. Jane Tregarron would stick to what she knew. Clinging to the fringes of gentility, that's what she knew. Nothing higher. A better prepared lady could have the pleasure of John Mandrake's icy hand and frosty bed and be welcome to it.

Jane felt the cold start to penetrate her woollen cloak as heavier drops of rain began to fall from the leaden sky. She turned back to face the Tregarron House standing above her on the cliff top.

Mines and a good marriage pushed the Tregarrons up to the ten-roomed house built by her grandfather. It was apart from the town and the only house that overlooked a small little-used cove known as Smith's Cove. They ate off Wedgwood china ordered from an illustrated catalogue. They were schooled in reading and writing. The females of the family played the pianoforte. Her father made sure her brother, Thom, practised his arithmetic.

Yet Jane needed new boots. They had been patched and mended but wet seeped through to her feet. She and her mother and three sisters all made lace but it was long hours of work for little reward. And now in winter less was done as it was impossible to do by candlelight.

And it was fortunate that Thom had paid attention to his arithmetic as Papa and he had gone today to Falmouth to see about employment for Thom as a clerk to one of the shipping merchants. Thom needed to work because money was so short. And she and her sisters needed to marry.

Marriage to John Mandrake would mean a house where she would be mistress. Comforts. Once she wed it would clear the way for her sisters. That times were hard Jane could see: from the food they ate to the fact that all their servants had been dismissed except one, their housekeeper, Mrs Beresford.

No reason was compelling enough to allow John Mandrake to take her as his bride.

Oh! If only he would show some consideration or kindness towards her! Then she might be reconciled to the fate they had decided for her. Why was she fated to have stirred the interest of such a cold, unfeeling man? 'He will make a good husband,' Mama had said.

Jane shivered. She could not be joined to such a man. Nor could she return home yet. Not until the rain and the wind had chilled her anger.

She fixed her gaze down on to the rocky path and trod carefully, avoiding the slippery stones. She pushed forward into the rain as it drove into her, stinging her cheeks and plastering loose tendrils of her hair to her face.

The path sloped downhill and twisted to the left. One of the steepest parts, Jane knew she had to take care for the next few yards until she was past the corner. The raindrops stung her eyes. Her view blurred. She put her hand on a rock to steady herself. She blinked hard to try and clear the water from her eyes.

She stepped on a loose stone. It slid away downhill carrying her foot some inches. Her balance wavered. She tried to grip the rock better. She fell, backwards.

Shock tremors from hitting the ground hard coursed up her spine, and then a sharp pain. Jane heard herself crying out. The gulls screeched their cries in return. She was falling some- where else, too fast. Into blackness.

Yet the gulls were still screeching. No, she was not in bed. Too hard, cold. Her face was wet. Jane opened her eyes and found herself looking up at lead-heavy clouds. Rain pelted her cheeks, chin, nose, forehead.

She took deep breaths and willed the pain to go away. It did not. It shot up her back in waves; waves that did not subside.

Time must have passed. She remem- bered falling on the path. How long had she lain there? How could she be able to move?

After some moments she managed to turn enough to be able to take hold of two tufts of hardy grass from the bank beside her. Jane clenched her teeth together. Tears pushed through as she tried to haul herself to her feet. The pain seemed hardly bearable.

She managed to pull herself up

somehow before she fell back unable to sustain the effort. She lay back on the damp grass. She shut her eyes.

She would be soaked to the skin. And then perhaps develop a fever. She'd had fever before. A terrifying time when she seemed to have lost half her senses and her whole being seemed to be burning up.

It hardly mattered if tears joined the other water on her face. At least her tears were warm.

★　★　★

On the southern coast of Cornwall, less than a day's ride away from the most westerly point of England at Land's End, lay the small town of Penhaven, trapped between the sea and tall cliffs.

This was Daniel Locke's description of the town to an American gentleman he met quite by chance in Lisbon. Grey-whiskered and of middling years, the gentleman's intent appeared uncertain. He paced the harbour-side, an agitated look in his eyes, asking the persons who passed him by whether they might tell him which ship was next bound for England.

'The Portobello, sir,' Daniel called over.

'Come here, young man, if you please.' The gentleman looked him up and down as he approached, squinting to keep the sun out of his eyes. 'Well, you're respectable-looking enough, I daresay.'

'Yes, sir.'

'I have a letter I wish to send home to England, to my sister.' He raised his bushy eyebrows. 'Tell me, whereabouts in England are you from?'

Daniel told him.

'Ah, Cornwall.' The gentleman smiled. 'The Cornish are smugglers, fishermen, miners or pirates. Which are you?'

'His Majesty's Navy, sir.'

'Yet of low rank, I perceive. Can I trust you?'

'I am a gunner, sir. His Majesty's Navy trusts me with its powder. However, I'll show you to HMS

Portobello and you can hand your letter over to the Master in person, sir.'

'No, no.' The gentleman drew a thick missal bound with string and wax from his pocket in his coat and passed it directly into Daniel's hands. 'You take it for me. And should you ever leave the service and want to come to the land of opportunity, come and find me, Galen King, Plymouth, Massachusetts.'

Mr King opened his purse to find the customary coin for the errand.

'My pleasure, sir.' Daniel backed away. He walked swiftly. The gentleman called after him. 'Galen King, Merchant. Plymouth, Massachusetts.'

Daniel did not turn around.

It was warm. The air was still. Quiet enough that a man might hear the click of his own boots. Damn foolish pride! Who was he, Daniel Locke, to turn away from an honest-earned coin?

It was a surprise effort of will, like none he had known hitherto, but he did turn back. And how that seemingly insignificant decision had altered the course of his life again. This time for the better.

He could hear his heart beating in his ears, but all his eyes could see now was a velvety black. It was cold. The wind howled, rattling the window casements.

He was no longer in Portugal, not even in his mind.

Daniel opened his eyes and stared at the plain distempered wall. Beneath his hands were the cool sheets of the bed. He lay in the small upstairs chamber in the cottage he'd once called home.

Outside raged a storm, pelting shards at the window panes. The rain distorted the pale light of late afternoon into a darker grey. Thunder rumbled.

The wind would be pulling slates from the cottage's roof, no doubt. They'd always picked up the smashed remains from the ground after a storm as fierce as this.

Yet all felt still.

He lay in a bed, not a bunk. A house did not pitch and heave. He was not aboard ship.

12

When he had arrived at his aunt's cottage this very feather bed had reminded his bones how weary they were, tempted him into long slumbers. When he'd woken it had been to wholesome food, and then he'd slept the more. It was only now, two full days later, that he had begun to feel vigour again but he had begun pacing up and down until he had noticed that his steps played the floorboards like fingers on a pianoforte's keys: a creaking melody that irritated him, and he had lain down again on the bed.

He had tried to cast his mind towards other things: what his aunt downstairs might be doing. Baking or sewing. Some other household task. What might be cooking on the stove for their supper.

His mind was not wont to linger on themes domestic. He recalled portions of voyages he'd long forgotten. Tiny episodes of memory that held no individual significance, but as a whole perhaps they meant something in his history.

He'd taken the letter from the Mr King in Lisbon aboard the Portobello, but when he saw it bore an address in Portsmouth, where they were bound, he kept it. He would deliver it in person, and overrule his foolish pride when the gentleman's sister offered to pay him for his trouble.

She paid him handsomely. Not in coin, but in employment after he got his discharge. Her husband was also a merchant. He stayed in Portsmouth for nigh on a year, assisting her man of business with every errand he was too important to run himself.

Outside, the storm had grown quickly, its violence forcing him back to the present.

And with that returned the questions he had not yet considered fully, questions he did not yet have an answer to. He had stayed in Portsmouth long enough. The time he had waited these long years for had arrived.

Daniel got up and pulled the wooden box from under the bed. He drew out the brace of pistols and held them as if they were a pair of new-born pups.

He would have a fortnight to think on it they had said before he should come back to them with his decision. Was it really a desire for justice that moved him now, or a baser motivation for revenge? Did it matter? In the meantime he had this pair of pistols, handed over to him without the asking of any kind of surety.

Daniel cocked one pistol, feeling the smooth metal of the lock hard against his thumb. It was unloaded yet he still found himself pointing the weapon towards the window.

Old habits die hard.

He had not yet gone down into the town where he would be seen, and recognised, and some would say, look thee at that Daniel Locke, the smuggler returns. His name would be forever tarnished here, though there were others who had got away who lived here. One man in particular.

He placed the pistols back in the box and the box under the bed. He walked downstairs and paused only long enough to pick up his hat and pull his boots on.

'Daniel?' His aunt bustled out of the kitchen. She wiped her hands on her apron. 'Daniel, mercy me! Are you venturing abroad in this weather?'

He drew back the bolt on the front door and lifted the latch.

'Take your greatcoat, Daniel,' she said. ''Tis only on the peg there, see.'

Daniel shut the front door behind him. His greatcoat remained indoors safe on its wooden peg. He wanted to be out here, and feel the wind and rain against him. Not be cosseted from it any more.

If any from Penhaven saw him, so be it.

★   ★   ★

'Miss?'

Jane started. A shadow appeared over her.

'Miss?' the voice repeated. It was

16

smooth, calm but with an understandable veneer of concern. But he was someone she did not recognise. Who could it be?

'Miss? Are you all right?' A hand touched her forearm.

Jane turned her head. A young man crouched beside her, the wind tussling his damp, ash-coloured hair. A tall man with an aquiline nose. Something in the strong line of his jaw was familiar. His high cheekbones. His nose.

There was little chance of a real stranger being here. No one came to Penhaven without reason. Had she lost her memory? Who was he?

'I slipped,' Jane said. 'I'm all right, thank you.'

His eyes regarded at her closely. 'Can I assist you?'

'Thank you . . . ' A wave of pain came and went, interrupting her thoughts.

'You plan to lie here awhile and admire the sky?'

Jane couldn't help smiling. 'There are enough grey clouds passing across above me to be entertainment I think.'

'Ah. And there was I about to offer you some company.' He leaned back, resting his elbows on his crouched knees. He wore drab woollen breeches, calf-high brown leather boots and a high-crowned hat with a buckle. His boots were highly polished. New boots, she was sure.

'You know this ground is thoroughly wet?' he said.

'I didn't choose to fall over,' Jane heard herself say before she had the wherewithal to bite her tongue. She had no reason to be piqued with him. Perhaps if she had been less hasty, she would not have fallen.

'I think, if you can stand, I should help you up. Let us at least find somewhere dry for you to recover?'

'I'm sorry.' Jane swallowed. 'I'm not feeling completely all right. When I fell, it hurt and it's still painful.'

'Here.' He stood up. The swallow-tails of his dark grey coat flapped in the breeze. He leant her his arm. Rain splashed down on to the stones of the path behind him.

He gripped her under both her arms and pulled. Strong arms; muscles like rock beneath her touch, Jane suddenly felt shy about holding on to him. He was a stranger after all.

Jane put her weight again on her feet. Her ankle felt as if someone was trying to press a red-hot iron rod into it. She clenched her teeth. 'M . . . my ankle!'

She found herself sagging against him unable to force her feet to stand. The front of her cloak brushing the front of his jacket. She swayed backwards, to get her balance. Failed and fell forward so that her chest pressed into his.

'I'm all right.' Jane caught her breath and tried to ignore the pain. 'I can walk.'

'Are you sure?'

Still he held her.

'Yes . . . ' She did not dare test her ankle again. 'No.'

'Will you let me carry you?' he said.

'There is no shelter here.' No, the cliff tops were barren; wind wrestled over the grass.

'Y . . . yes.' Tears pricked at the back of the eyes. All Jane could think was that she could lie on a soft bed until the pain subsided.

He reached down and picked her up, putting one arm beneath her legs and the other around her back. As effortlessly as she was a feather pillow, or so it seemed. It felt safe to be in his strong arms.

She tried to forget that he was a stranger as it made her feel uneasy although her instincts told her he was someone she could trust.

2

'Home,' Jane murmured. She rested her head against his chest and felt the warmth from him ease some of her chill. Was this a dream?

'Where is your home?' His voice seemed very gentle. He could not be a stranger. Although how such a handsome man should have escaped her notice she did not know.

'Who are you?' she said.

'It's your home I need the direction of.' He seemed to shake his head. 'My name is of no matter.'

He walked forward, on to the path. It was unspoken that he'd make sure she got home safely.

'I live at Tregarron House.' The wind chipped at her words.

'Tregarron House is some way farther up, is it not?'

'Yes.'

A pair of gulls circled overhead, calling out to one another. Jane shivered. She was soaking wet. She turned her face into his coat. It was still raining but at least he seemed to know where Tregarron House was, even if he had not told her who he was.

Jane blinked the rainwater from her eyes and glanced up. She could see the underside of his chin and then a curious view of his nose and the rest of his face. He could not have shaved today and his skin was weather-beaten. He was a man used to being outdoors, like the fishermen. Yet he did not dress like a fisherman, more like a clerk or a well-to-do farmer. And he was better spoken than most. That was it! He worked in a gentleman's trade though he was no gentleman.

'Do you live close by?' she asked.

'Yes . . . and no,' he said and still did not volunteer his name. 'Are you acquainted with Mrs Locke?'

'Yes, I am.' Mrs Locke was a kindly widow and her small cottage was only some yards away, tucked next to the road just before the right hand corner before the incline of the hill turned sharply towards Tregarron House.

'Good. I am taking you there. Do not be concerned. 'Tis not far.'

'Mercy me!' Jane heard Mrs Locke's voice. The cottage door creaked open. 'Come in, come in! You'll catch your death out there.'

He carried her inside. A blazing fire filled the room with an orange glow. Immediately the warmth began to reach her skin.

The door was closed behind them and Jane heard the scraping sounds of the bolts being fastened.

'What has happened?' Mrs Locke said.

'I slipped and fell.' Jane turned to see Mrs Locke's eyes regarding her closely. The lines on her forehead were deep. 'If it is possible might I shelter here until the rain is over? I'm so sorry to trouble you — '

'Hush your modest ways! Now, you

can sit down or lie down? It might be a little cold upstairs as there is no fire lit, though I can soon see to it.'

'It's only my ankle, I think. I can sit down.'

'Here.' Mrs Locke said to her rescuer.

Jane caught a glance of Mrs Locke pointing towards her old wing-backed chair in front of the fire. Mrs Locke clearly knew the man well. She would not have allowed him to walk directly into her cottage otherwise.

It would be revealed soon enough, Jane decided and concentrated in case she had to do anything to assist as he put her down gently in the chair. He seemed to manage without her help. She found herself sat in the chair perfectly comfortably. Her ankle still throbbed but she felt warm and her face and hands had already begun to dry.

He stepped back as if to survey his efforts, smiled and his whole countenance changed from an expression of seriousness to one of openness.

'Jane, are you comfortable?' Mrs Locke brought over a well-stuffed cushion and placed it behind her back. 'Can you take your cloak off? It will be soaking wet without a doubt.'

'Yes, thank you.' Jane struggled out of her cloak. She found herself watching the stranger closely. He threw his coat on to the back of another chair and stood in his shirt-sleeves. They stuck, damp, to his arms.

Did he live here? With Mrs Locke? There could be no other explanation for his state of undress. Yet Mrs Locke lived alone. How could that be?

Mrs Locke handed her cloak to him. He placed it on a peg on the wall.

'Thank you,' Jane said. Then, feeling that some explanation of her accident was necessary, said, 'I'd seen the sky was darkening but I misjudged it would begin to rain so quickly.'

'There, there. It'll pass soon enough.' Mrs Locke came forward and patted her hand.

'And thank you, sir,' Jane said to the stranger.

His eyes met hers. They were a strange mixture of colours: new wood with flecks of green and grey; eyes that had seen more of the world than she ever had.

'You've met Daniel, my nephew, before?' Mrs Locke said. 'Did you not recognise him? He has grown fine and tall since you would have last seen him.'

The stranger was none other than Mrs Locke's nephew, Daniel, now a grown man. She had not recognised him.

'I'm pleased to make your acquaintance again, Mr Locke,' Jane said.

'Thank you,' he said, his tones rich and deep. 'But I have not yet discovered your name, Miss . . . ?'

'Miss Jane Tregarron,' Mrs Locke said.

'Of course,' he said. He looked amused. 'From Tregarron House.'

'I remember you as a boy on the beach.' Jane was not sure she had just said that but she did remember him. He must have been fifteen then, she six or seven. He'd been tall then, with the same nose but with a shock of hair whereas now his hair seemed flatter. Or perhaps it was the effect of the rain.

The children in Penhaven used to congregate on the beach in the afternoons and play games with the sea and the sand. Daniel had been one of the leaders, and different somehow. Even then. And then, not long after, he'd gone away to sea they'd said.

'Fourteen years,' he said as if answering her unasked question. Jane wondered if her memories matched his. Did he even remember her from those days? 'Fourteen years in His Majesty's Navy.'

He took a seat close to the fire. His face should have been warmed by the glow of the orange flames but remained rigid, without a smile. 'And now I'm home.'

'I'll put the kettle on,' said Mrs Locke. She disappeared into her kitchen.

Jane found that she was not sure where to look, or what to say.

'Jane . . . ?' he said. 'You played on the beach too as a child?'

'Yes,' she replied. So he did not remember her after all.

'You had a brother did you not?'

'Yes, one brother. Thom.' It was with Thom she'd gone out to play. None of her sisters had been old enough to be allowed out then.

'Older or younger?'

'A year older than I.'

The lines at the corners of his eyes deepened. 'Yes . . . I remember. And Thom now?'

Jane couldn't help the warm feeling in her chest at the news that he did indeed remember, even if it was only of her brother. Thom used to run after the older boys wanting to join in their games if they would let him.

'Thom is twenty and is at home with the rest of the family. Though . . . ' She stopped. She would not tell him that likely as not Thom would soon be leaving them to work in Falmouth. 'And I have three sisters also. All younger. Our house is only a few minutes walk on from here heading up towards the cliffs.'

He nodded and gave no sense that he was curious that she had not finished what she had started to say about her brother.

Mrs Locke brought in the tea. It scalded her tongue at first, but warmed her inside and Jane found herself looking at Daniel Locke as if he was the most interesting thing in the world. He was not, she chided herself, but then again his life had been somewhat unusual.

She was sorry when it was time to go. He rose to assist her but she tested her ankle and it seemed ready to bear her weight. She walked home alone. It was hardly far, which was a pity. She would have liked more of his company.

★   ★   ★

Later, as she walked up the glistening steps to the back door of Tregarron House, Jane remembered. The wind had dropped but the sky remained stubbornly thick with smoke-coloured clouds. Daniel Locke had gone away to sea to avoid a worse fate: being convicted by the magistrate of smuggling.

Her father had been a magistrate for a while, until his health had made it impossible. He had not been a magistrate then, but he might know what had happened that day fourteen years ago.

Yet she could not condemn Daniel Locke. Not yet. The Tregarrons might have been smugglers once, or pirates. There could hardly be a family in Penhaven which had not at some time turned to smuggling to improve their fortunes. It was hard to feed a family from fishing alone.

She let herself in through the back door. It was ordinarily left unlocked during the day. The kitchen was empty. Heat came from the oven. Mrs

Beresford, their cook and housekeeper, had not gone far. Jane walked through into the hallway. Empty. No sounds came from any of the rooms, nor upstairs. It was as if the house was deserted. Impossible.

The door to the parlour was ajar. She pushed it open. Sitting where they all would were they working lace were Mama, Charlotte, Harriet and Georgie. Every pair of hands was empty. Mrs Beresford sat in the old wing-backed chair in the corner. Papa and Thom had returned home. They stood in front of the fire, their hands firmly tucked behind their backs.

Every face looked pale, not itself. Papa's was like a milk jug that had been drained of its last drops. Even Thom, who always broke silences with an observation or intelligent remark. Thom stared at the plaster cornice in the middle of the ceiling, his eyes unmoving.

The china clock on the mantelpiece chimed the half hour.

Mama spoke. 'Jane, what took you so long?'

'I was caught in the rain, Mama.' Jane felt she was speaking too quickly. She tried to slow. 'I had to wait until the rain had stopped, and — '

'You're here, that's all that's of consequence now.' Her father's voice was uncharacteristically sharp. 'Sit down, Jane. I have something to say to all of you.'

Mama pulled a handkerchief from her sleeve and dabbed her nose. Jane removed her cloak which was still damp and sat down on the chaise next to Charlotte.

'As head of the family . . . ' Papa cleared his throat. 'On occasion it falls on the head of the family to shoulder unpleasant burdens. This is his duty no less, to protect the family in so far as he is able. However, sometimes, a burden increases to the magnitude whereby it may no longer be hidden. This is our situation and this is why I can keep it from you no longer. Be assured that it is only in the gravest of circumstances that I do this.'

A sob broke from Mama. She pressed her handkerchief against her mouth and stifled herself. Mama could be vexing, or vexed. But she never cried.

Jane felt seized with cold. Yet the fire blazed. Her stomach doubled-up inside itself, as if someone was trying to clutch it.

Whatever it is, Jane thought, Mama knows. She drew a deep breath and concentrated on listening to her father's words.

Creditors, loans . . . She didn't at first understand what he was saying. As he continued she perceived it was truly grave.

'It is unlikely that we shall be able to continue to live here for much longer,' her father said. 'The house must be sold.'

A curtain moved, disturbed by the draft coming in the window. Ordinarily Mama would tut-tut. Clicking her tongue against her teeth she'd go and check that the window latch was secured properly. Mama did not move. No-one spoke.

A thin smile appeared on her father's face. It appeared an effort to him. 'Let us have no more on this now,' he said. 'And let none of this yet go beyond ourselves. All is not quite lost. Things may yet not turn out so bad as they seem. But we must all be cautious and we must all economise wherever we can.'

There would be no new boots, Jane found herself thinking and felt unworthy to have had such a selfish thought. She'd always seen her father as an upright man, intelligent and unselfish. He would not have spoken to them all as he just had unless it was true and the house had to be sold.

She'd noticed economies in the kitchen, and these had become stricter in recent weeks. And Mama had been imploring them to work longer hours at their lace making.

Supper was eaten in near silence. It

was only later after they had retired upstairs to bed that any of Jane's sisters spoke. And then in hushed whispers.

'What does it all mean?' asked her younger sister, Georgie, her eyes wide. She had dressed for bed in her white, calico gown. In her hand she held her horsehair brush but she made no attempt to brush her hair.

Jane took the brush and dragged it slowly through Georgie's long, dark locks. The rhythm might sooth her youngest sister, she thought. Or even herself.

'We have yet to see,' she said. 'But events may yet turn in Papa's favour. He was only speaking of the worst possibilities.' Jane was not sure she believed what she was saying. She turned to another subject, determined that she could bring a smile to her youngest sister's face. 'Do you remember last week we talked about putting on a new play?'

'Oh yes?' Georgie's eyes seemed to brighten. 'The one with the princess?'

'Yes, that one, where you would be the princess. It's not long until Papa's birthday. Do you think we should rehearse and it be a surprise for him?'

'Yes!'

'I'm sure we can get Charlotte and Harriet to agree, don't you think? You ask Harriet when she comes. But it needs to be a secret, mind, if it is to be a surprise for Papa.'

Georgie settled down in the bed that she shared with Harriet. Jane tucked her in and turned to go to her own bedchamber which she shared with Charlotte. She spoke to Charlotte about the play.

'Yes, perhaps we might do that,' Charlotte replied, though her thoughts seemed to be elsewhere. 'Papa would like it.'

Later, when they were both in bed, Charlotte extinguished the taper. The only light in the room came from a sliver of silver moonlight allowed in by the gap where the curtains did not draw together properly.

'Jane, are you awake?' Charlotte whispered. From the other bed came deep breathing. Their younger sisters were asleep.

'Yes.' Jane turned around to face her sister. Enough moonlight came in through the gap in the curtain to show that Charlotte's cheeks were streaked with tears.

'Circumstances must be very bad,' Charlotte said. 'Papa would have avoided telling us if he could.'

'Yes.' Jane kept her voice low. 'But events may yet turn.'

'They will for you.' Charlotte's voice held a touch of bitterness. 'You can marry John Mandrake and that way secure your own future. But what of the rest of us? Of Mama and Papa, or me, Harriet and Georgie?'

Jane felt gooseflesh prickle her neck. An image of John Mandrake appeared in her mind. He had dark, severe hair, cut very short; no softness there. His eyes were grey; they glittered like granite but they never smiled. His mouth was always drawn taut, his fingers fiddled with his cuffs, the only movement as the rest of his body always seemed completely straight and unmoving.

John Mandrake had paid her some attentions some months ago, enough to give rise to some speculation but Jane had never encouraged him because he made her feel cold. He had never brought a smile to her lips or any feeling of pleasure. The Mandrakes were the richest family in Penhaven and John Mandrake was the heir. Marriage to John Mandrake should be her boat on the horizon; the vehicle to rescue her from all this. But the idea of being John Mandrake's wife, of being bound to him, gave her only strong feelings of unease.

'Marriage may not be the answer,' she said.

'Better a loveless marriage than the workhouse.' Charlotte's voice was tight.

'Don't talk flummery.' Jane turned away. The time did not feel right to confide her deeper feelings with regards to John Mandrake with her sister. 'I'm going to sleep now. Let us talk in the morning.'

Jane nestled into her pillow. In her heart she knew that Charlotte spoke a truth. Making lace could not keep a whole family. She pulled the blankets right up to her chin but in the depths of her bones a coldness had set in.

In the middle of the following morning Jane went into the kitchen. Her stomach rumbled. She'd hardly eaten the evening before and breakfast had been meagre, simply porridge, dished out by Mama who had given each of them only one large spoonful though Papa had got the extra scrapings.

Mrs Beresford stood with her back to her. She banged pans and dishes making a terrible racket.

'Mrs Beresford?' Jane said. Mrs Beresford seemed in a temper. Should she ask whether there was anything she might do to help?

Bang, clatter, bang. Mrs Beresford gave no indication she had heard her.

'Mrs Beresford?' Jane said more loudly.

Mrs Beresford turned around. 'What you be wanting?' she said, her tone unfriendly. Quite unlike the Mrs Beresford Jane had known for many years.

'I was just wondering if there was anything I might eat?' Jane said.

'Well, I'll be wondering where my wages are to come from next,' Mrs Beresford said. 'Since I'm to leave here.'

'You're leaving?' Jane forgot her hunger.

'Eleven years I've worked here and this is the thanks I get!'

They were having to let go of Mrs Beresford? However bad she had imagined things were last night, things must be far, far worse.

3

'Things must be bad,' Jane muttered. She did not know what to say to Mrs Beresford at all. Sorry hardly seemed good enough.

'Bad they are to tell a loyal servant you won't be paying their hard earned wages — '

'Mrs Beresford!' The door to the kitchen opened and in came Georgie and Harriet.

'Mrs Beresford?' Harriet smiled and looked up at her expectantly.

'You've come for your biscuits, have you?'

'Yes, and Mrs Beresford, guess what we are to do for Papa's birthday this year?' Georgie said. 'A play! And Harriet and I are to be princesses in it, aren't we, Jane?'

'A play? Your papa will like that.' Mrs Beresford reached into a cupboard and pulled out an earthenware jar. She doled out two biscuits each. 'There you are, and not a word to your Mama. She'll think I'm spoiling you.'

'No, Mrs Beresford. Thank you!'

'Run along now,' Mrs Beresford said.

'Truth is,' she said to Jane when they had gone, 'there's nothing but a spot of honey to sweeten them. I started making these oaten biscuits for Harriet and Georgie when they started coming in here complaining of being hungry. Poor mites. And now you've come in for the same!' Mrs Beresford handed her two of the substantial biscuits before putting the jar back in the cupboard.

Jane tucked them in her reticule.

'Well, I shan't be leaving today if that's what you're thinking,' Mrs Beresford said. 'I'll keep a roof over my head 'til it suits me.'

When they'd started making lace Mama had let them keep a portion of their earnings. Jane had only ever spent a small amount of the money on some ribbon. The rest remained in a small

cloth bag she'd made to house it —
some seven shillings and ninepence.
Should she give some of this money to
Mrs Beresford? She wanted to, but the
thought struck her, if things were this
bad would her own family starve?

'Will you go to your sister?' Jane asked.

'I'll have to.' Mrs Beresford let out a
sigh. But she had a sister who lived the
other side of Falmouth. It was unjust
that Mrs Beresford would not be paid
what was owing to her but at least she
had somewhere to go.

'I'm sorry,' Jane said.

'Ah, my love.' Mrs Beresford smiled.

She wanted to be alone, to think, and
outside away from the house she could
eat the biscuits undisturbed. Jane
fastened her grey woollen cloak up to
her chin before stepping outside. She
would take the coastal path. She often
walked here, either with her sisters or,
like today, alone.

There was a prodigious feeling of
space being on the cliff top with the sea
below and the sky above. The morning

was bright but a few grey clouds sculled above. Jane quickened her step.

She saw the events of yesterday in her mind as vividly as they were happening again: coming into the room of silent faces; hearing her father stumble over what he had to tell them; Mama's tears; Charlotte's tears later.

Where had her own tears been?

As if she'd conjured them from nowhere she felt pricking at the backs of her eyes, heat, and then her vision began to go hazy. She did not realise she was crying until she felt the drops slide down her cheeks.

She wiped her sleeve across her eyes but it was only temporary relief. There was no one to see her here. She could cry, if she wanted. She was not sure what she was crying for, yet, except the knowledge that whatever came to pass, things would never be the same again.

She sat down on a piece of rock in a sheltered spot that looked out to the sea and wiped her eyes with her handkerchief. Beyond Penhaven Cove the coast was cracked and unpredictable. A lighthouse should be built. Some boats took their chances; the shallow bays and caves were too irresistible to be passed over if your trade was in goods not for the eyes of the Revenue.

Jane put her handkerchief away in her reticule and drew out one of the biscuits. She ate it too quickly. The second one, she savoured, and considered again the thought that had come to her fleetingly in the kitchen. She had seven shillings and ninepence safely tucked away in a cloth bag at the bottom of the blanket drawer. It was not enough money to feed the family for long on its own, but what if it were invested? Invested in goods that could be sold profitably. How did other families in Penhaven survive?

However, she did not know who in Penhaven were responsible for the free trade.

'Miss Tregarron? Good Morning.'

Jane looked up to see him standing before her; Daniel Locke. Today he wore a heavy great coat that seemed almost too big for him although he was a tall man. Apart from that he matched her memory from yesterday. Jane found herself smiling as her eyes met his.

'Good morning, Mr Locke.' She swallowed the last biscuit crumbs. He had a deep gaze. There was something in the way that he looked at her that she liked.

'You are fond of the outdoors?' he said.

'Yes.' Could he be teasing her? Jane was not sure.

'And you have not caught a cold?'

'No. That is fortunate. I might have done had I not been . . . rescued. Thank you.' She wanted to tell him of what had happened yesterday after she had come home, but she could not. No one outside the family could know. Because of the shame of it. 'Thank you,' she repeated. 'Sincerely.'

He smiled; in his eyes as well as with his lips.

'You look quite comfortable on that

rock,' he said. 'Not in any hurry to get anywhere. It must be that you are here only for your own pleasure?'

'You have perceived my motive, in part.' She looked at him because her eyes would not let her do otherwise.

'And the rest?' His mouth hardly moved as he spoke.

'The rest I cannot tell you. It is sufficient to say that there is harmony in nature. Out here I am soothed by the presence of the sea, the land and the sky.'

He sat down on a rock not three feet from her. He leaned forward, closer still. 'And what if there were a storm?'

'Then I should get very wet.'

'Now you are teasing me,' he said. He straightened himself up. 'It may surprise you to learn that you are not the only one to have troubles. Mine concern a struggle of conscience. There are where-fores and whys, but the substance is not important now, although perhaps I shall explain it all to you someday.'

'What is of interest is that yesterday

there was a storm here, and it was in the heart of that storm that I wanted to be. As if somehow, by pitting my own self against it I could conquer another, different storm inside me.'

'Oh.' Jane struggled to think what to say. She understood, she thought, at least partly.

'A foolish notion,' he continued. 'But how glad I was that my foolishness turned out not to be completely in vain, as had I not been out in the storm I would not have found you. And here we both are, and remarkably in good health with not a sniffle between us.'

'Yes.' Jane smiled and he returned her smile.

'When I was younger, I was full of regrets. Too many missed opportunities. Pride and fear held me back from so many things. Not now. I am different now, or I would not be speaking to you thus.'

'You will make the right decision,' Jane heard herself say.

'I daresay I will.' His smile had

weakened and she sensed that part of him was somewhere else. And then he changed the subject. 'I suppose you have always lived in Tregarron House?'

'Yes. All my life.'

'How strange that that should feel curious to me now. I, who should have never left this place myself. Think, what if I had grown up only yards from you, all these years, where would we be now?'

'We would have been friends,' Jane replied. She knew as instinctively as she knew the ebb and flow of the tide that this would have been so.

'Perhaps we may yet.' He stood up. 'Though my time here is short.' He raised his hand as he made his way back on to the path. 'Goodbye.'

She did not want him to go, and she wanted to ask him what he meant when he said his time here was short. And what he meant when he said, had I not been out in the storm I would not have found you.

He was gone, walking up the path

and out of sight before she could muster her thoughts together. Jane pulled off one glove and felt her cheeks. They were burning.

She sat on the rock for a few moments. Images of Daniel Locke filled her thoughts. She could not think of a time when another person had intrigued her so.

She could not sit here all morning. She got to her feet and walked home.

She unlatched their low front gate.

'Jane!' Georgie rushed out of the house. 'You will never guess! Papa has gone out unexpectedly and Mama has gone with him. Shall we rehearse the play now?'

All her musings about Daniel Locke fled her mind and a host of worrying reasons of where Papa and Mama might have gone to crowded in instead.

Jane tried to join in with her sisters and pretended to be enthusiastic about the play. But she could not wholly take her mind off their troubles, so severe that Mrs Beresford was to leave them.

She would not tell any of her sisters today. Mrs Beresford had certainly said nothing to Georgie.

Jane found out later that Papa and Mama had paid a call to the Mandrakes. Mama was smiling when they returned and even Papa looked a little less as though he carried the weight of the world on his shoulders.

'Jane! Charlotte!'

Two days later Mama swept into the parlour where they were sitting and waved a letter at them. 'We are invited to the Mandrakes! The Lord is merciful! Jane you must . . . you must take this opportunity to pin that young man. And Charlotte, a younger son may not be so bad. Not now.' Mama's face fell.

'Yes, Mama,' Charlotte said.

Jane held her tongue. Mama was right that she should use this chance to try and finally secure an offer from John Mandrake.

A year ago Mama had been convinced that Jane was close to receiving an offer of marriage from John Mandrake. Although he was accustomed to avoiding dancing, he had danced with Jane on a succession of occasions. He had shown her particular attentions.

What he had never done was attempt to engage Jane in any kind of conversation beyond fripperies.

He might not have had what Jane considered to be a conversation, however, his sister, Diana, had fallen ill and the Mandrakes' house had been closed to visitors for months. Until now.

'I'd heard in church that Diana Mandrake has recovered from her illness,' Mama said. 'Your father and I went to pay them a call as soon as we heard. And now we are invited there! How fortunate that she should have recovered at last. Jane, we must make sure that you look your very best. We must pray that he has not forgotten you these past months. Fetch your dress! Your best dress!' Mama clapped her hands together. 'Quickly now! Oh Jane, you had better try it on.'

Jane walked up the stairs. Charlotte followed. She could not quite summon up her mother's enthusiasm. It was a chore, not a pleasure.

Her best gown hung at the back of the tall mahogany wardrobe she shared with all her sisters. As she pulled it out she noticed how the light reflected off the satin. Ivory-coloured, the dress was in the Empire style with a high-waist and tiny, puffed sleeves. She had made the dress less than a year ago from a plate in a fashion magazine.

Charlotte had wanted a similar dress so they had traced the pattern and had used it to make her a dress of pale blue satin with an overskirt of sarsenet.

She tried the dress on. Charlotte helped her to fasten it.

'It still fits, which is a mercy,' Charlotte said. 'Now help me try on my dress.'

'Quickly, then Charlotte because Mama is waiting.'

'I have need of a husband too.'

Jane bit her lip and helped Charlotte into her dress. It fitted and Charlotte smiled at herself in the mirror on the dresser.

'Oh Charlotte, you can preen yourself as much as you like but help me get unfastened please first.'

'Yes, madam.' Charlotte gave a mock curtsey.

Jane stepped out of her dress and carried it carefully downstairs.

Mama immediately set to work to sew some new lace to trim the sleeves. 'Apart from that it needs no more adornment,' Mama said. 'The beauty of your dress, Jane, is in its simplicity.'

Jane wound Mama's leftover thread on to a piece of card. Yes, the dress was beautiful. She had worn it to a soiree at the Mandrakes. It might have been the dress which John Mandrake noticed that evening before he first paid her attention. She'd worn the dress to supper parties and had planned with Charlotte for the evening that never came where they would go to a subscription ball in Falmouth.

These past few months had been quiet. There were only a handful of families in Penhaven with which they might socialise and the Mandrakes were at the centre of everything; the most important family in Penhaven.

★　★　★

Jane breathed in deeply as Charlotte pulled her laces tightly.

'There you go,' Charlotte said. 'My turn and then I'll help you fix your hair.'

Jane stifled a yawn. They'd been up with the sunrise every day for the past week working on lace as if their lives depended on it. Perhaps it did. They'd only stopped a short while ago this afternoon so that they could get ready for the Mandrakes' party this evening.

Charlotte turned around and Jane fastened her dress, tying the yellow ribbons of her bodice in a neat bow.

Both their hair had been tied since

yesterday evening with rags that they'd slept on and not yet removed them. Jane now sat down in front of the dresser and mirror and Charlotte untied the pieces of calico. Her curls tumbled free. Charlotte picked up their ivory comb and pulled the curls at the sides of her head forward carefully. The rest she swept back and pinned into a loose bun.

'Jane! Charlotte!' Mama's voice came calling from outside in the corridor. 'Are you ready yet?'

'Surely we're not leaving yet?' Jane said feeling Charlotte's hands still.

'Come in, Mama,' Charlotte said. Jane felt a pin scrape against the back of her head as Charlotte hurried to finish.

The door swung open with a creak.

'Gosh, Charlotte, your hair's not done yet! Heavens! Sit down and I will do it.'

'No, no, Mama, Jane can do it perfectly well.'

'No. No.' Mama shook her head. 'Jane, go downstairs and ask Mrs

Beresford to serve tea in the parlour. With some thinly sliced bread and butter. Or cake if there is any.'

Serve tea in the parlour ... It was like how things used to be.

'And see if Harriet and Georgie are ready,' added Mama as she left the room.

Jane went across the corridor to her sisters' room and found Harriet brushing Georgie's hair. It fell limply across her shoulders.

'Did you not keep your rags in?'

'Rags don't make any difference,' Georgie said and burst into tears. 'I'll never have curls.'

'There, there.' Jane put her arms around Georgie's shoulders. Her youngest sister was only fifteen. At that age having one's hair exactly right really mattered. She added, 'You look very pretty whether you've got curls or not. Both of you hurry up though. Mama wants us to have some tea before we go.'

Jane found Mrs Beresford and then she came back upstairs to get her reticule. Charlotte was ready and so they went downstairs to the parlour leaving Mama to pester the younger girls.

'You had better snare John Mandrake tonight,' Charlotte said.

Jane looked at her sister. Charlotte stood up tall, seemingly bound within the lacing of her dress. Her expression was set firm, her lips and eyes were unsmiling. She must be thinking of her own situation as much as Jane's. Perhaps the situation of the whole of the family.

4

The Mandrakes' house was in Penhaven itself. Set back from the sea in it's own large gardens it may well have began its life as a modest dwelling, but it had expanded over the generations. It's most recent addition was a grand frontage in the neo-classical style. Three rooms had been knocked together to create a long withdrawing room and widen the entrance hall.

As near as anyone in the neighbourhood had to a ballroom, it was here that the evening party took place as twenty families and a trio of musicians from Falmouth crowded in. There would be dancing this evening and . . .

Jane's thoughts stopped short. She was standing in the middle of the vast room with her parents and sisters. Just entering the room was a party she did not recognise, apart from one gentleman —

Daniel Locke! He was standing with his back to her. She regarded his broad shoulders and grey hair and wondered what he was doing here at the Mandrakes. It didn't seem credible somehow.

She took a sip from her glass of ratafia. The evening seemed to sparkle with something, whereas minutes ago it had promised to be flat.

Daniel Locke turned around. Jane stopped herself from gasping out loud.

The nose was wrong, too thin. And the eyes, the whole shape of the face. It wasn't Daniel Locke at all! Some other gentleman whose countenance was unfamiliar to her. How could she have been so foolish as to imagine that Daniel Locke would be here at the Mandrakes'.

Mrs Locke was a good woman who had always been friendly to Jane and her sisters, but Mama would never have called on Mrs Locke except for charitable purposes. Mrs Locke was simply not of the same rank in society.

Except it was the Tregarrons who had

need of charity now. Jane crushed that thought and made sure there was a smile on her face.

'Jane?' came her Mama's voice. 'Jane, have you not heard a word of what I've been saying?'

'No, Mama. I mean, yes, Mama. What were you saying?'

'Hush, lower your voice. Look, John Mandrake is over there. We must make sure you talk with him and dance with him this evening. Come with me.'

Mama led the way, fanning herself vigorously. The small circle of people parted to allow them through to where John Mandrake stood by the french windows.

'Mr Mandrake,' Mama gushed. 'It has been such a very long time.'

'Mrs Tregarron.' He bowed. There was a stiffness about him that Jane found reminded her that this was a man she struggled to find likeable. Yet she was supposed to marry him! She opened her own fan. It felt hot.

'And Miss Tregarron.' He bowed in

her direction but did not catch her eye or smile or give her any real sign that he acknowledged her presence.

'And dear Diana? How is she?' Mama asked.

'Yes, she is here this evening.'

'Oh I have not yet seen her!' Mama flashed a girlish smile. 'Is the dancing to begin soon, Mr Mandrake, for my dear daughter, Jane, loves to dance. Do you not, Jane?'

'Yes, Mama.'

'When the dancing begins I would be honoured to dance with your daughter, Mrs Tregarron.' Still he did not catch Jane's eye. He gave another small bow. 'And now if you will excuse me?'

'Of course, of course. Come along, Jane, we must pay our regards to dear Diana.'

'Mama,' Jane said as soon as they were alone again, and with reproach in her voice.

'Hush, hush. Now don't forget to smile, and especially when you dance with Mr Mandrake later.'

Later came too quickly.

'We might dance the Cotillion, Miss Tregarron,' he said, interrupting her conversation with Mrs Harris. His eyes seemed to be hooded. 'If you are willing?'

Mrs Harris smiled at him and backed away.

Jane had no choice but to assent. 'I am honoured, sir,' she added.

'Honoured? Nonsense! You and I are friends, are we not?'

It was perhaps the first pleasant thing he had ever said to her. They walked into the centre of the room to join the other couples.

The musicians played and they danced. Jane took care to smile. Mr Mandrake danced well.

After the dance he led her out of the drawing-room. 'If you don't mind,' he said. 'I think we have something to discuss.'

He took her to another room that led off the hallway, a small square-shaped parlour with sofas. He motioned for her to sit down. He sat opposite her. She wasn't sure whether to be relieved or concerned.

'You must know at least in part what I am about to say?' he began.

Jane smiled but did not reply.

'I thought to ask you some important questions,' he said. 'But Diana's sudden illness put many things on hold. I hope you do not think badly of me?'

'No,' Jane said. 'I did not think that.' She'd not considered he had spared any thought to her at all. But Mama had been right. She hardly dared imagine what he would say next.

'I wanted to ask you whether you would be my bride?' There was a pause before he continued, 'I ask it of you now. If you say the word I shall ask permission of your papa tonight.'

'I do not know what to say.' Jane battened down her surprise. But something didn't feel quite right. After all this time, what was the hurry? She wanted to ask him, but didn't dare.

'Say you'll be mine.' There was an

urgency in his voice.

'This has come somewhat as a surprise,' Jane said. 'Might I kindly ask that I may give you my answer tomorrow?'

Something flashed across his face. Anger? Of course it would not occur to John Mandrake that anyone would refuse him, anyone in Penhaven certainly, for he stood to inherit the largest fortune in the town. Indeed why should she refuse him? She had no reason.

'Of course,' he said. 'I will call on you tomorrow afternoon.'

He might have said something of his finer feelings, given some indication that there was some passionate reason why he wanted her as his wife. He did not. He said, 'And I expect your answer will be favourable. I suspect your parents have not informed you of our bargain?'

What bargain? Jane stared at him. She could read nothing from his face.

He gave a small smile that chilled her. 'No, I see that they have not. Our marriage will mean that they can continue to live in comfort. I'm sure you understand me?'

Jane gave a nod. What she understood was that her hand in marriage had somehow been sold to John Mandrake.

He took his leave of her saying that he hoped she would enjoy the remainder of the evening.

She was left alone in the Mandrakes' parlour. Unlike theirs at home that had lumps in them, the sofa was comfortable. Their mantelpiece was littered with ornaments whereas at home theirs was nearly bare. What had happened to the China figurines they used to have? Had they been sold?

John Mandrake offered her the opportunity to escape from all that and more. He'd said that her family's future would be secured. Yet still she hesitated.

She started at the loud sound of voices from the hallway. He had left the door ajar. She recognised one voice immediately — Mrs Harris.

The Harrises were in mining and Mrs Harris held supper parties to which they were occasionally invited, and had lent Jane and Charlotte some magazines with fashion plates from which they had got inspiration for their dresses.

'Have you heard?' Mrs Harris said. 'Mrs Locke's nephew has returned.'

'Yes,' another lady replied. Jane could not recognise who it was. 'I saw him in the market square. Gave me quite a turn. We can do without his sort round here.'

'Went a boy, came back a man,' Mrs Harris said.

'Once a bad sort, always a bad sort. They should have transported him when they had the chance.'

'Ah, but there's many round here involved in the trade, my dear.' Mrs Harris had lowered her voice. By the trade Jane knew she meant smuggling.

'I don't condemn it if there's families to feed,' said her companion, 'but that Locke boy put lives in danger for his own ends. We all know what happened.'

I don't, thought Jane. She'd only been a child at the time. She couldn't imagine Daniel Locke wilfully putting lives in danger.

The voices drifted away. Mrs Harris and her companion had moved on. Jane rose and made her way back to the drawing-room. She kept a smile fixed on her face and tried to enjoy the rest of the evening. She managed to ignore Mama's curious glances, and when they got home, escaped to bed before she could be questioned.

She listened to Charlotte's even breathing beside her. Charlotte had had a good evening. She danced with several young men Mama had told her were eligible enough. Before, Mama had had high ideas. Now, Jane thought, Mama would be happy for Charlotte to marry anyone who could provide her a home.

Outside the wind gathered pace. The windows rattled. Jane could not sleep. She wondered if there would be a storm.

After some time, it quietened and

Jane heard the hoot of an owl. She stepped softly out of bed, went over to the window and drew back one of the curtains. The night was clear. Stars twinkled like diamonds in the black sky.

A perfect night to take a boat over to Guernsey and come back laden with profitable contraband.

Jane knew what she was going to do. The idea had been forming in her mind as she'd lain in bed unable to sleep. If there was the smallest chance that she could do something to escape having to marry Mr Mandrake, and yet make sure her family did not starve, she must do it.

She ignored the tremble of her hands as she dressed quietly and thought instead of the small cloth bag with the money she'd saved from lace-making.

She was going down to Smith's Cove to listen to the calming sounds of silence and the waves, and to watch if any boats came in tonight so she could see who was plying the trade in Penhaven these days.

What she would do with that knowledge she was not yet quite sure, but the trade was how others had made their fortune and her small nest egg might be her opportunity.

There was enough light from the moon to make her way down the path and to the beach at Smith's Cove. She would not have taken a lantern with her anyway as she did not want to draw attention to herself. The cold pecked her cheeks. She could hear the sound of her own breathing.

The night was safe, but occasionally men consumed too much tavern ale and stumbled home. Occasionally there was trouble. Not tonight. It was too late. Penhaven was abed. The taverns had closed hours ago. In another hour or two the first fingers of dawn would appear in the sky.

She crouched behind a group of dark rocks and watched the shore. All was still for a while. Her legs grew stiff but she did not move.

At last she was rewarded with the

splash of oars. A small fishing boat, bobbing like an upturned shell, made its way through the dark water towards the silver beach.

The boat neared. Two men jumped out. Jane could not discern their faces. The breeze stole their voices away from her, although they spoke in low tones. They pulled the boat ashore. A third silhouette handed over square crates and boxes from the boat. They carried these along the beach and out of Jane's sight. To a cave or other hiding place she guessed.

On his way back to the boat one of the men passed very close by to her. Jane kept absolutely still, hardly dared to breathe. He turned his face towards the cliffs and she caught a glimpse. She recognised the deep-set eyes and high forehead of Leonard Castle, a fisherman from Penhaven, and a smuggler. There could be no doubt what the three men who had landed goods in Smith's Cove in the dead of the night were up to.

A strong hand clasped over her mouth and pulled Jane backwards. Within a moment, before she had time to realise what was happening to her, she found herself on her back pinned against a masculine body behind her that held her, one hand holding her arms fast and the other over her face.

'Hush,' a male voice said.

She could hardly move let alone speak. Jane felt her chest rise and fall. At least she could still breathe. And strangely she felt no fear or panic. She was no threat to the smugglers and she had coin to put their way to prove her good faith.

After some moments Jane felt the grip in which she was held slacken. He said, 'Who are you and what are you doing here? I'm going to let you speak now but answer me properly now. If you scream there is no-one to hear you in any case. The boat has gone.'

He removed his hand from her mouth.

Jane took a gulp of cold air.

'Answer me,' he said. His tone sounded kindly enough, but Jane had no intention of giving her name if it could be avoided.

'It is no business of yours,' she said finally.

'Miss Tregarron?' He let go of her fully and stumbled away. Cold air enveloped her where his body had been. She watched him as he stood up straight some feet away from her and pulled his hand through his hair. Daniel Locke.

'Mr Locke,' she whispered.

Daniel Locke on the beach at Smith's Cove in the night. Of course Mrs Harris had said he was a bad sort. Nearly convicted of smuggling, he had, so she should hardly be surprised.

'What are you doing here?' The tone of his male voice made clear his confusion.

'I can't tell you,' she muttered. She wasn't ready to share her reasons yet. It was not that she did not trust him. Strangely she did. But she'd rather deal with an ordinary fisherman like Leonard Castle than Daniel Locke.

'Are you mixed up in this business?' He frowned.

'No.' It was not a lie.

'But you were watching the boat come in?'

'I was curious.'

He stood all the while watching her. Dawn was not far off, Jane thought. She must get home. She stood up slowly. He made no move towards her. She spoke. 'I could ask you what you are doing here, and what gave you the right to think that you could manhandle me.'

'I cannot tell you that either,' he said. His eyes were veiled, prepared to give nothing away. 'But I can see you home?'

She nodded. They walked in silence back to within sight of Tregarron House. She stood a while watching him walk away back towards the Locke's cottage before she crept back into the house and into bed and woke a short while later with the others. She was still yawning at breakfast. Mama attributed her tiredness to the Mandrakes' party.

After breakfast Jane sat in the parlour with her sister and tried to concentrate on winding some new thread on to a bobbin. The last thing she wanted to do was sit all day making lace, waiting for Mr Mandrake's promised afternoon visit.

She wanted to go and see Leonard Castle. That could bring in better financial rewards than an hour or two of lace making even if she could not yet tell Mama or Papa what she was doing. But she needed an excuse to leave the house and go to Penhaven.

Jane found Mama in the kitchen with Mrs Beresford. What she needed was an excuse to go into Penhaven but she'd only been a few days ago to take their lace to Mr Hargreaves. Perhaps something was needed from the shops?

'We're out of salt, Mrs Tregarron.' Mrs Beresford shut the cupboard door. She didn't need to think up an excuse now, Mrs Beresford had just provided her with one.

Mama bustled past Mrs Beresford,

opened the cupboard door and took down the brown enamel jar. She looked inside.

'Not so much as a pinch left,' Mrs Beresford continued, her hands on her hips. 'Not even enough for a loaf.'

Mama's eyes looked downcast as she replaced the jar. 'We shall have to buy some more to bake today.'

'I'll go, Mama,' Jane said.

'Yes.' Mama sounded distracted. 'But we only need a farthing's worth. Just for the bread.'

'Yes, Mama.'

'Take Georgie with you, she might do with some fresh air, she's been looking a little pale.'

Jane opened her mouth to protest but couldn't think what to say. This was her opportunity to try and speak to Leonard Castle. That was going to be difficult if Georgie was to accompany her. She would have to think of something.

'Are you going to marry Mr Mandrake then?' Georgie asked as they walked down to Penhaven.

'Yes.' Jane heard herself say. 'In fact Mr Mandrake said he would call on me this afternoon. So let us hurry and get this errand over with.'

Outside the shop Jane drew Georgie to one side. 'I need you to do me a good turn.'

'What's that?'

'Can you go into the shop and buy Mama's salt?' She drew the copper farthing Mama had given her from her reticule. 'Then wait for me here. There's someone I have to go and see.'

'Mr Mandrake?' Georgie's eyes lit up.

'No, not Mr Mandrake but it's very important and you are not to tell anyone about it.' If Georgie could keep quiet about Mrs Beresford's biscuit jar then she could keep quiet about this. 'Promise me.'

'All right,' Georgie agreed although her expression did not look wholly happy. 'You'll be back soon?'

5

Is fate a force like a black stallion running wild and out of control? Daniel considered. Or is it simply a case of chance, like gambling dice thrown by hand?

Weak sunlight cast patterns across his aunt's oak table. He paused, holding the brass ladle he'd been polishing. Not two or three minutes ago, he'd glanced up and towards the window. An idle movement, nothing more.

Walking past the cottage at that same moment, Jane Tregarron, and with her a younger girl he supposed to be one of her sisters. Both hurried, heading in the direction of Penhaven.

He could not deny that there was something about Jane Tregarron. Something beyond her sea-blue eyes, that had first arrested him. Rather it was something in the way she held herself in the face of adversity. Some part to her character that he could not help but admire.

He had no right to admire her, less to get up and follow her as if she was some ill-doer. He intended to remain in Penhaven with his aunt a week more. No longer. Yet he ignored his own good sense and reason.

He caught up with them in Penhaven town, as Jane went one way and the other girl another. He followed Jane, keeping far behind her, for a short way. She turned the corner and he had to wait. She would see him if she turned around.

She did not. She walked straight ahead with determination and stopped at the front door of one of the sea-front terraces. Daniel could not recall who lived there. And he could not see who opened the door. His jaw stiffened.

Jane Tregarron slipped inside the cottage.

He turned around immediately, in time to see her companion disappear into Curnow's shop.

So old Mr Curnow still kept his mean little shop after all this time. Daniel hesitated. Mr Curnow might not be pleased to see him. It was fourteen years ago but he had been one of that fateful expedition who had been caught. The only one to have been caught, in fact, for the man he'd gone out with that night, Leonard Castle, had managed to escape. Managed to escape by leaving Daniel to choose between being drowned or being caught.

Daniel felt a tightness in his chest. Leonard Castle was a coward and a traitor.

The failure had fallen on his head alone. Their contraband cargo of tea and tobacco had ended up in the hands of the Revenue, and not as intended in the hands of some of Mr Curnow's private customers.

It was fourteen years ago, however.

Daniel pushed the door to Curnow's shop open.

★ ★ ★

The Castles' cottage was in the next street, one of a terrace. Jane knocked on the stout door not really knowing what she should say nor what to expect. The door was opened by a young woman wearing a long, white apron. 'Yes?' she said.

A small child tugged at Mrs Castle's skirt. She bent down, picked up the child and rested him or her on her hip. She looked Jane directly in the eye. 'What is it you want?'

'Is Mr Castle at home?'

'What would you be wanting with him?'

'I cannot say out here on the street,' Jane replied. She knew she'd not yet introduced herself. If she could manage not to, so much the better.

'Come in.'

Jane followed her into the small cottage. Like the others in the same row, it had just one room on each floor with a small lean-to extension out back.

'Mr Castle's not home so you better tell me.' Mrs Castle made no offer to Jane to sit down.

Mrs Castle must be aware of her husband's nocturnal activities. What wife would not? Jane decided to take the risk. Her only other choice would be to speak to Daniel Locke and she did not want to have to do that.

'I have some money I'd like to invest,' she said. 'In goods.'

Mrs Castle smiled. 'Ah. Well, do you want to sit down? Would you like a cup of tea?'

Tea which had never had duty paid on it, Jane found herself thinking. She said, 'No, I cannot stay, my sister is waiting for me.'

'Can you come back later?' Mrs Castle asked.

'Not today, but I can tomorrow or the next day as soon as I can. Here.' As a gesture of good faith Jane drew two shillings from her reticule.

'I'll see he puts that into something for you.' Mrs Castle took down what looked like a tea caddy from the shelf, unlocked it, placed the money inside and carefully locked it again. 'He takes half the profit. He's the one risking his neck and all.'

'Yes,' Jane said.

Mrs Castle drew a small cloth-bound book from a drawer and a pencil and wrote something inside it. 'There, written down. And your name?'

'Jane.' How interesting that Mrs Castle should be able to write, Jane thought. Did half of Penhaven come to this unassuming cottage and have their spare shillings and pence taken and faithfully recorded by Mrs Castle? Mrs Castle acted as if it was all very regular.

'Jane . . . ?'

'Jane.' Mrs Castle might not know her but she would certainly know of the Tregarrons.

Mrs Castle shut the book and put it away. 'That's all done then.'

Jane felt her heart thud. At the worst she'd lost two shillings but what excited her was the prospect of actually making some profit. If so, she'd give the Castles the rest of her money.

'Thank you. I must go.' Georgie would have finished in the shop by now and be waiting for her. The last thing Jane wanted was for Georgie to kick up some dust and break her promise to keep quiet.

But Georgie was not waiting on the corner of the street where Jane had left her.

Jane looked around her, back towards the cottages and houses, out towards the harbour and the sea. Was Georgie still in Mr Curnow's shop? Jane hastened her step.

Mr Curnow looked up from where he stood behind the counter as she entered the shop.

'Jane!' Georgie smiled and rushed forward towards her. 'I'm sorry. We were having a conversation. I have the salt.'

Another person stood in the shop. Daniel Locke.

'Will you be wanting anything, Miss

Tregarron?' said Mr Curnow.

'Only my sister, thank you.'

Daniel Locke's eyes held hers. The dark wooden fitments of the shop seemed to frame him.

'Miss Tregarron,' he said in a quiet voice.

'I see you have met my sister, Georgiana.' Jane held her hands together behind her back. She tried to look away at the dusty panes of Mr Curnow's windows, at Georgie, at anything except his grey eyes.

'Indeed,' he replied.

'Mr Locke is Mrs Locke's nephew,' Georgie said. 'He used to live here, Jane, but — '

'But what is he doing in Mr Curnow's shop?' Jane said before she could stop herself.

'Buying twine.' He smiled.

The door creaked open. A woman bent hunchback over a dark walking stick shuffled in from the street.

'Those days were long ago,' Mr Curnow said. He nodded towards the old woman. 'Good day, Mrs Kernick. You have a long memory, don't you, Mrs Kernick? You remember this young man here?'

Mrs Kernick raised her head. Her eyes, like a pair of wizened currants in the face of a gingerbread man, took Daniel Locke in.

Her lips quivered. 'Locke's boy,' she mumbled. 'A bad one.' She raised her stick. Her voice rose, and wavered, like a small boat too close to rocks, so it seemed to Jane. 'Away with 'ee, boy! Away with 'ee back where 'ee belongs, wi' the devil. Not here.'

Daniel Locke's countenance whitened.

Mr Curnow stood still, his eyes taking in the scene. He does not know what to say, Jane thought. She wondered why this should be.

Mrs Kernick rapped her stick against the wooden floor. 'Away with 'ee I say.'

Georgie's hand found her way into Jane's.

Daniel Locke took off his hat and gave Mrs Kernick a small bow. 'Good day.' He left the shop without another word.

* * *

Mr Mandrake arrived at Tregarron House at exactly three o'clock. Jane found that she was trembling as Mama welcomed him into the parlour.

He was dressed smartly, like a country squire with tan coloured breeches and a finely tailored dark blue coat. She supposed he was as good as a country squire so far as Penhaven was concerned. He sat down on the sofa opposite her, taking care to flick his coat tails out of the way so that they would not be crushed.

He had not chosen to sit down next to her at least, that was something. Jane hazarded a smile but he did not seem to notice, his eyes were fixed on Mama as she poured the tea using their best china.

Jane swallowed the small piece of vexation that rose in her chest. Perhaps he was simply not an observant man. Unlike Daniel Locke, a voice inside her whispered.

Having finished pouring the tea, Mama made a transparent excuse to leave them alone together and left the parlour, shutting the door quietly behind her.

Jane clasped her hands in her lap and waited to see what would happen next. It was not for her to say anything or try to lead this conversation.

Outside the sun had broken through the clouds and was shining. It warmed her back and created window-pane-shaped patterns on the carpet.

Mr Mandrake coughed.

Jane looked at him, tracing the edges of his countenance. The corners of his eyes and his forehead held creases that made him older than his years. In other circumstances she might have felt a little sorry for him. He appeared a joyless man but perhaps this had been wrought by hardships. He might be wealthy but his sister, Diana, had recently been gravely ill.

'Miss Tregarron.' He met her gaze. 'There is only one reason why I am here and that is to ask you whether you would consent to become my wife.'

The patterns of light on the carpet faded. The sun had gone behind a cloud.

'Yes, Mr Mandrake, I will consent to become your wife.' It sounded so formal, but this is what it was, little more than a transaction of convenience.

'Thank you, Miss Tregarron, you have made my day.' A half-smile played on his lips. 'You must come up one day very soon for supper and we will agree the practical arrangements.'

'Yes, of course.'

'There is no reason to delay the wedding is there?'

'No.' Indeed there was every reason to hurry it so that he might seal his bargain with Mama and Papa and everyone could live happily ever after.

'Then I shall see the rector and arrange for the banns to be called without delay.'

'Thank you,' she said. If they called the first set of banns immediately she might be married three weeks from now. Mrs Mandrake, wife of John Mandrake of Penhaven.

'Now let us share with your family the good news,' he said and rose.

Jane felt as if she was somewhere else. A seagull soaring above in the sky, looking down on the scene where Mama and Papa, Thom and her sisters crowded into the parlour and John Mandrake accepted the congratulations due to him and shook hands with each of them in turn before taking his leave of them all, and then as if nothing out of the ordinary had happened, Mama urged them all to take up their cushions and continue making lace.

'Take Charlotte with you,' Mama said the following day, 'and show her what she must do.'

It remained unspoken but it would be Charlotte who would take responsibility for taking the lace to Mr Hargreaves after Jane was married.

Mist had settled, cold to the touch and spectre-like, half-shrouding everything even into the afternoon. There seemed no reason to delay further; the mist would linger all day. Jane and Charlotte dressed warmly and walked down to Penhaven.

Jane stopped in the street some way before Mr Hargreaves's house.

'We must wait until the street is clear,' Jane explained. 'For we should enter Mr Hargreaves's house unseen. The back of his house is down that alley there, the next one, but we had better wait here until that woman has gone in case she sees us.'

'I see,' Charlotte said and pulled her shawl more tightly about her shoulders.

They waited for a woman carrying a basket to walk around the corner out of sight and then proceed down the narrow alley that had high walls of dark grey stone on either side; the sides of buildings without windows. Seemingly unbroken but only a few yards down they came to a high wooden gate in the wall that Jane unlatched.

The gate led into a large yard hanging with sodden washing despite the day. Jane ducked under the washing to the back door of the house and knocked.

Charlotte followed and stood behind her while they waited.

Mrs Hargreaves answered the door. Her sleeves were rolled up and the scent of starch and soap wafted out of the house.

'Ah, Jane,' she said. 'Come in.'

'This is my sister, Charlotte,' Jane said.

Mr Hargreaves came into the kitchen at his wife's request. Jane handed over the lace. It never took long, a simple transaction only. Mr Hargreaves inspected it quickly, taking a pair of spectacles from an upper pocket that he put to one eye. Then he measured it for length, made a quick calculation using his fingers and then paid her for it, taking the money from a drawer in the sideboard.

'My sister, Charlotte, will bring out

lace in future,' Jane said.

Mr Hargreaves nodded but did not speak. His wife showed them out.

'Is he always like that?' asked Charlotte as they trudged up the hill.

'Yes. Pay no heed of it.'

Home came into sight, and also a lean black horse tethered outside.

'A visitor?' Charlotte muttered.

From the house, the sounds of raised voices. The front door swayed backwards and forwards, unfastened. Something was very wrong. Jane quickened her step.

They reached the house as a tall man, smartly dressed and clean-shaven, stepped outside. He raised his tricorn hat to them and said, 'Good afternoon.'

Papa appeared in the doorway, holding on to the frame with one hand as if he was unsteady on his feet.

'Jane? Charlotte?' Mama's voice came from inside. Jane saw a figure behind her father. 'You're home, are you?'

'Yes, Mama.' Jane answered.

The visitor mounted his horse in one movement, without assistance.

'Papa?' Charlotte ran to their father and took his spare hand in hers. Jane saw that Papa's face was pale. His eyes stared yet he did not appear to be looking at anything in particular.

The visitor flicked his reins. The animal broke into a trot. Its hooves clattered. He rode away down the path, veering to one side to avoid a man stood some way down the hill looking up at them. Daniel Locke. Jane felt her heart thud in her chest. What had he seen?

'Who was that, Papa? Mama?' she heard Charlotte ask.

'The Sheriff's Officer.' Papa's voice sounded strange. 'Don't worry, my love, we've paid what we owe in taxes.'

'And now there is no money left!' Mama's voice was raised. 'None! You fool!'

Jane stood and watched Daniel Locke. At first he did nothing but now he was walking up the hill slowly towards them.

She turned around. 'Mama, take

Papa indoors. This has all been a terrible shock. Let us all have a cup of tea. Charlotte, go and ask Mrs Beresford to put the kettle on.'

She sounded so in control, Jane was surprised at herself. Perhaps she had it in her to carry off being Mrs John Mandrake after all.

For now all she needed to do was make sure that Daniel Locke had not witnessed their visit by the Sheriff's Officer, and if he had, she must try and persuade him to keep the knowledge to himself. If word got out . . . If people knew . . . it didn't bear thinking about.

6

Daniel Locke stopped walking when he saw her coming. He stood fast on the granite hillside as substantial as the town of Penhaven below. Wisps of smoke came from cottage chimneys and disappeared into the damp air. The breeze ruffled Daniel Locke's hair and clothes but he remained standing motionless.

Jane glanced behind her to see that Mama, Papa and Charlotte were making their way indoors. She lifted her skirts a few inches and hurried. Better if she dealt with Daniel Locke herself than faced a questioning after.

'Mr Locke!' she called as she came within earshot of him.

'Miss Tregarron.' His eyes seemed to convey a tapestry of emotions but she could not pull out any one in particular. 'The Sheriff's Officer has been?'

That dashed some of her hopes as surely as a helpless wreck stuck on the rocks would be broken further by the action of the sea.

'Yes,' she confessed. He must have recognised who the visitor was, she supposed. And there were only a few reasons why a Sheriff's Officer would come all this way, and none of them were good news.

'Is there anything I can do?' He paused. 'To help?'

'Oh, no.' That was unexpected. What could he do anyway? Nothing she could ask of him. Not loan her money, if he had some and she doubted that. Besides, they were near strangers.

'Please,' she said. She licked her lips and tasted salt. 'Please keep what you have seen to yourself. For now.'

'Yes, I will.'

Perhaps he could help her. Jane's instinct told her that Daniel Locke was a man she could trust, despite his reputation as a smuggler. There were doubtless plenty of folk in Penhaven involved in smuggling who led perfectly respectable lives besides. Like Leonard Castle.

'Perhaps you can help,' she said. Jane had no idea what she might say next.

Daniel Locke stepped forward. If he reached out now, he might touch her. 'Are you all right? You look pale.' He looked as if he was about to say something more but stopped himself.

'A little shocked, perhaps.' She tried to smile but couldn't. And it was Papa and Mama and her sisters who would face the worst of it. She was safely on her way to being married to Mr Mandrake and that would take her away from it all.

'Might I . . . hold you?' He stepped even closer. His arms came around her before she could think to pull away. She pushed her face into the darkness of his jacket and felt the rough material against her cheeks. Tears pricked. She pushed them back.

She felt something brush against an ear. His hand? He tucked a curl that had escaped from under her bonnet behind her ear. She wanted to sink into the place that was only inhabited by him. There was no place in the world she would rather be now than this.

That shocked her. She pulled herself away, allowing the sharp cold of the air to embrace her instead. It felt unnatural but she ignored her feelings and thought instead about propriety: the wrongness of a woman allowing a man to whom she was not closely related or betrothed to embrace her.

John Mandrake had never held her.

Daniel Locke took a step backwards, his head cocked slightly to one side. He watched her, his lips parted as if he would say something.

'I must go,' Jane heard herself say. She wanted to cover her embarrassment and the quickest way would be to leave.

'Let me help you.' His voice was steady. 'Meet me later. Tonight?'

'Not tonight.' All she wanted to do this evening was bury her head in a pillow and sleep. To fall asleep would be such a balm. It erased all problems for a while.

'Early in the morning? Before anyone is awake.'

'Not tomorrow,' she said. 'The day after.'

'Smith's Cove?' he suggested. 'After dawn.'

Jane came indoors to see Papa carrying a large, worn-looking bag down the stairs. He placed it down by the front door. Behind him came Mrs Beresford wearing her coat, buttoned up to her chin, and her best straw bonnet. She carried a tied-up blanket, stuffed full with something. Her possessions. She was leaving them.

At the base of the stairs in the hall, Mrs Beresford turned and faced her papa squarely. Jane thought she had never seen Mrs Beresford look so fierce. At the back of the hall stood Thom, Charlotte, Harriet and Mama, watching silently.

'Jem, he's a good lad, is coming with

the cart to take me to Falmouth,' Mrs Beresford said to Papa. Her tone sounded weary. 'I'm not asking for myself but to give the lad something for his trouble.'

Papa did not answer immediately.

'I'm not asking for myself,' Mrs Beresford repeated.

'Of course,' Papa muttered.

Mama hurried forward. 'Wait! No! He'll only spend it at the inn on rum and shrub.'

'That's his business,' Mrs Beresford said.

Jem was a labourer at Halkett's farm. Jane was sure he was a good sort. Most men drank did they not? It did not violate their characters. It was Mama who seemed to be acting out of character. Her eyes looked wild and she spoke with a desperation which made Jane want to run forward and comfort her as if she was the mother and Mama the child.

'Will he take you to Falmouth without payment?' Mama said to Mrs

Beresford. 'It's that we — '

'No.' Papa sounded firm. 'Three or four pence. We can spare that.' He reached into his pocket and drew out a small handful of coins, mostly pennies and ha-pennies.

'Papa?' Charlotte's voice sounded thin and reedy, but beneath it was a thread of steel that Jane recognised. Charlotte could be determined when she wanted to be. 'I have a small amount of money — '

'Hush!' Mama turned to Charlotte and put her finger to her lips. 'Papa is dealing with this. Come on girls, let us go into the parlour.'

Mama had control again and Jane reluctantly followed her into the parlour. She tried to catch Mrs Beresford's eye to show her how sorry she was but she couldn't. Mrs Beresford's attention was fixed on Papa and the money he was counting out.

They sat down in their usual places, Mama, Charlotte, Harriet and Jane. Mama began handing out their lace cushions as if it were any ordinary afternoon. Jane found herself thinking that Charlotte must have saved some of her lace money, just as Jane had done.

For a moment Jane wondered whether she could involve Charlotte in her financial plan. She decided against it. There was too much of a risk still. If something went wrong she might never see those two shillings again, let alone a profit.

'Where is Georgiana?' Mama said.

No-one knew.

'Shall I go and find her?' Jane said. Georgie was probably upstairs engrossed in a book. She loved reading, even reading the same stories over and over again.

'Yes, please, Jane,' Mama replied.

Jane felt glad to leave the parlour. The hall was empty. She walked upstairs but Georgie was not in her room. She glanced out of the window and saw Mrs Beresford sitting upright on Jem's cart, her face obscured from view by her firmly secured straw bonnet. Her bag and tied blanket of possessions sat on the cart behind her.

Jane watched from behind the curtain as the cart pulled away and headed jerkily down the hill towards Penhaven, and then Falmouth. Then it struck her. They would all see. Everyone in Penhaven would know that Mrs Beresford had left them.

She sat for a moment on her bed. The iron rail was cool to the touch. Part of this was for Mama and Papa to deal with. For now, she just needed to find Georgie.

She looked in the kitchen. Thom sat at the kitchen table eating a wedge of bread. He did not look happy but a small smile came to his face as he looked up. 'Jane? Oh Jane, it's all so terrible. I shall have to get employment somewhere, shan't I? As a clerk I suppose, in Falmouth.'

'Yes,' Jane said. She supposed he would. 'But you are good with figures.' She found that she did not want to think that Thom would be leaving them soon too. 'Thom, have you seen Georgie?'

'No. Not for a while.'

Thom stood up and stuffed the remains of the bread in his pocket. Jane could tell from his look that he was thinking the same as she. They both knew their youngest sister well. Georgie was either oblivious; in her own world somewhere on the cliffs tucked away and probably reading a book; or she was upset.

They searched the pantry and the outhouse; in the dining-room and even disturbed Papa who was sitting alone with his head in his hands in his study. Jane went back to the parlour with a heavy feeling in her bones.

'Mama,' she said. 'Georgie is not in the house.'

'What? How can she do this to us? Isn't there enough going on?' Mama threw her lace cushion to the floor. Jane thought she saw tears swimming in Mama's eyes.

'Shall Thom and I look for her outside?' Jane said.

In the depth of her being, Jane felt

that Georgie was upset. Upset at the visit of the Sheriff's Officer, upset at the departure of Mrs Beresford, and even perhaps upset that her sister, Jane, had kept a secret from her.

'I'll go too,' Charlotte said and stood up.

'Yes, go. She'll be hiding somewhere, no doubt reading one of her books.' Mama put her hand over her mouth and stifled a small sob. 'Well, she should be working on her lace! And so should Jane and Charlotte rather than having to go out and look for her. Selfish child!'

'I'll stay and work on the lace, Mama,' Harriet said in a gentle voice. She picked Mama's blue cushion from the floor and began to untangle the bobbins that had gone awry when Mama had thrown the cushion down.

★ ★ ★

Thom took the path up towards the headland and suggested Charlotte take the path down the hill towards Mrs Locke's cottage, and Jane to Smith's Cove.

Jane did not want to go to Smith's Cove. There was no real reason — there would be no smugglers there in the middle of the day and she had even suggested she meet Daniel Locke there.

Better go to Smith's Cove than to have to walk past Mrs Locke's cottage, she thought. What if Daniel Locke spied her and thought she had come to seek him out? There was enough of an awkwardness between them for Jane to be unsure of her every action when Daniel Locke was present. He always seemed to watch her so closely.

Jane stepped on to the sandy beach. It glistened in the weak sunlight. The tide was out. The sand was flat beneath her feet, as if it had been combed. Yes, combed by the sea, thought Jane. Smith's Cove was a perfect secret landing place. Not only was it invisible unless you were on the cliffs immediately above, with the current tides the sea would eradicate any footprints or traces that a small boat had landed in the night.

Perfect for a secret meeting with Daniel Locke. She pushed that thought from her mind and concentrated on hurrying towards the caves in case Georgie had taken it into her head to hide in one.

'Georgie?' Jane called into the darkness of the first cave. No answer. She would rather not wander inside the cave if she could help it.

She tried the next cave. No answer.

The next cave involved clambering over some rocks.

'Georgie?' No answer.

Jane rested her hand on the rock. There were not other caves in easy reach. Not unless the tide . . . How long has Georgie been gone? No, she could not have gone to the far set of caves currently inaccessible with the sea lapping at their mouths. No, surely not.

'Georgie!' Jane called as loudly as she could. 'Georgie! Are you there? Can you hear me?'

'Jane!' came the faint reply. From the cave she stood outside of.

'Georgie!' Jane walked a couple of steps into the cave. 'Where are you?'

'I'm coming!' Georgie's voice was stronger.

Jane heard the sound of movement: footsteps.

'Jane!' Georgie appeared from the gloom and threw her arms around Jane's waist. 'Oh, you came and found me.'

'I wish I hadn't had to. What are you doing? Don't you know it's dangerous to be here by yourself?'

'Oh, oh . . . ' Georgie broke into sobs.

'Did you want to get away? From everything that is happening?'

'Yes . . . Mrs Beresford . . . and . . . and . . . '

'It's all right now.' Jane stroked her sister's hair. 'Come on, let us go home and let them know you are safe. Mama is very anxious about you. Everyone is very worried.'

'Jane,' Georgie said as they walked

back along the beach. 'In that cave there were lots of things.'

'What things?'

'Crates all stacked up.' Georgie swung her hand out wide. 'And boxes. And large barrels, fastened together with rope. And kegs.'

Crates and barrels? Smuggled goods! 'Perhaps someone has run out of room at their home to store things,' Jane said. It was not necessarily a lie. 'So they thought they'd use the cave. I am sure they will come back for their things when they are ready.'

Smuggled goods. Was this a place used by Len Castle or his confederates?

Later that afternoon a boy came up to Tregarron House with a letter. Charlotte caught him at the kitchen door, before he had a chance to come inside and see that they did not even have a cook or any servant.

Mama stared at the letter, her hands letting the stiff paper wilt, her eyes glazed. She read it out loud to them in the parlour.

Would Jane dine with the Mandrakes the following evening? Jane and her Mama and Papa. Thom and her sisters were not invited. The supper to make the wedding arrangements, Jane thought. Her mind suddenly filled with a blackness that made the lace pins, exactly securing the lace card to her cushion, seem to curve and contort.

Jane put her lace cushion down.

'Of course we shall attend,' Mama said. She opened the lid of the writing table. 'I will answer them directly.'

★ ★ ★

Jane woke far earlier than she needed to. Her sleep had been restless. She had been so pleased to find Georgie safe and well but Mama had given her youngest sister a sound scolding and Georgie had gone to bed early and in tears. Her mother was beginning to despair.

Unless . . . ? She pictured in her mind a dark cave filled with crates and

111

kegs. Merchandise of value. Perhaps merchandise she already had a stake in.

If it were possible to open one of the crates, could a small amount of the contents be removed without its loss being discovered. Could she? Even a small amount of tea, for example, might be sold for a great profit.

No, she could not steal. It was one of the ten commandments and completely wrong.

She lay in bed for as long as she could keep herself there. Finally, she got out of bed and pulled open the curtains. Sunlight streamed in. Charlotte stirred and gave a large yawn.

Marry John Mandrake as quickly as possible, a little voice in Jane's head said. That is the best way you can solve it all.

7

'I have some news that will please you.' John Mandrake spoke softly, leaning towards her. Jane took a small step back to put more space between them. His voice had a veneer she was unaccustomed to. 'I will tell you later,' he finished.

They were assembled in the Mandrakes' withdrawing-room, newly wallpapered with a sprigged pattern of tiny flowers. Mr Mandrake, John Mandrake and her father were all in dark evening clothes. Her father's seemed shabby. Mrs Mandrake wore an Empire style deep blue gown and a pearl necklace. They had recently tapered Mama's green dress to better reflect the fashion but by comparison it seemed old and out-dated.

Jane held her head high. Her own dress was her ivory satin, the same one she had worn to the Mandrakes' party, but it was as fashionable as the simple pale pink gown that Diana Mandrake wore.

'John.' Mrs Mandrake gave a wide smile. 'Will you do the honour of taking Miss Tregarron into dinner?'

'Of course, Mama,' he replied.

They followed their parents into the dining-room. Diana Mandrake followed them. It was an intimate party. John Mandrake had two brothers but they were away at sea, trading with the Empire. His elder sister had married. Only he and his younger sister, Diana, remained at home.

The small oval mirrors on the wall sconces reflected the flames of beeswax candles so that the dining-room bathed in a yellow gold. They discussed the arrangements for the wedding. It all came from the Mandrakes and Papa and Mama agreed with it all.

The Mandrakes would do everything from arranging to see about the calling of the banns to entertaining afterwards here at their house. All they need to concern themselves with was her wedding dress and her portion.

Her portion? What could Papa and Mama possibly afford to give her, Jane did not like to think. She tried to concentrate on eating the delicious food placed course by course in front of her by liveried servants.

John Mandrake sitting on the other side of the table gave her a smile she was sure was designed to be seen as encouraging. It was an effort to smile back. An effort because she would rather that sitting opposite her was Daniel Locke.

After dinner, as she had anticipated, John Mandrake found an excuse for them to remove from the company, saying that he wished to show her the Mandrake family portraits that were hung on the upstairs landing.

She had no alternative but to agree and follow him out of the drawing-room. He did not offer her his arm.

The carpet was plush beneath her slippers, the house well heated. There were only half a dozen portraits yet the sitters were universally stern against dark, murky backgrounds.

They stopped by the picture of the most unappealing man of them all. He seemed to stare at her from his canvas. Jane tried not to shiver. A man who bore an uncanny resemblance to John Mandrake.

'My grandfather,' John Mandrake said.

Jane thought of the portrait at home of her own grandfather. The painter had been a follower of Gainsborough and painted her grandfather against a summer's landscape.

'Once we are married, we will live at Tregarron House,' he said, interrupting her reverie.

'At Tregarron House?' Had she quite heard him correctly?

'Yes. My mother and father will continue to live here. It will not be permanent. I intend to build a new house. Out on the headland. With every modern convenience.'

'And what . . . what of my family?'

Jane could not help herself.

'Why, they are moving to Falmouth of course.' He gave a smile, if you could call the strange twist of his lips such a thing.

Falmouth? When? Jane nearly said. She bit her tongue. Jane was filled with revulsion and a great sense of unease. And uncertainty. Mama and Papa were moving to Falmouth?

His lips relaxed. His smile faded. Jane felt her heat beating against her ribs. He took her hand, lifting it and curling his fingers in hers possessively. Jane resisted the urge to snatch her hand away.

'You did not plan to go to Falmouth with them, did you?' he said. 'Naturally we will bring the wedding forward. Now that Diana is better, there is no reason for any delay. No reason at all.'

Was this their bargain with John Mandrake? Not only had they sold him their daughter, but their home, the house her grandfather had built.

'No,' Jane muttered. 'I mean, yes, of course. I had not really considered . . . '

she stopped. She did not want to say anything for it would all be untruths.

He let her hand go and half-turned away. 'Shall we return to the company?'

Her heart slowed. In all the times she had wished that John Mandrake would show some feeling towards her, she had never thought it would be like this. At the very same time as she felt closer to him as a human being that ever before, it only made her feel even more frightened of him. There was something about his manner, a coldness that went arctic-deep.

⋆   ⋆   ⋆

Late into the night while the rest of the household slept Jane was awake. She dressed, taking care to be as quiet as possible. Charlotte slept on, undisturbed. Jane left the bedroom and shut the door behind her slowly. It gave a tiny click. She tiptoed downstairs and let herself out of the back door.

The dark air pinched her face with

cold. Jane pulled her shawl tightly around her. She was only doing this because Daniel Locke said he would help her. No other reason. Not because he had held her and for one short moment, in his arms, she had felt that everything would be all right. This was about one thing only: the smugglers.

Orange streaks painted the sky. She walked down the steep path to Smith's Cove. All was quiet.

The waves ran up the beach, and then withdrew back into the grey sea. Jane walked across the beach to where the sand was damp. Farther on was the cave in which Georgie had hidden; where Georgie had seen the goods hidden. Jane considered if she dared take a look for herself.

She did not. She stared at the empty sea and listened to the familiar sounds of the waves chopping against one another.

'Jane?' He used her given name.

'Mr Locke.' He walked towards her, wearing his swallow-tailed dark grey coat she'd become accustomed to seeing him in.

Jane had plaited her hair but the wind pulled at it. She must look unkempt to him, not a well brought-up young woman. She wasn't sure why that mattered but it seemed to and she wished he would speak rather than simply standing in front of her looking at her.

'You agreed we'd meet so you could tell me,' he said at last. 'I saw the Sheriff's Officer visit, remember,' he coaxed. 'What is it?'

She wanted to tell him, but the right words did not seem to come to her. How she could explain that her family were now paupers when she did not understand how it even had come about herself?

The breeze tickled her neck where Jane had not fastened her cloak up properly. She gave a small shiver. His voice was the real caress.

Jane breathed in deeply. She said, 'You've seen it.'

'I saw the visit you had from the Sheriff's Officer. I chanced to be out and I could not help it.' He paused. 'I did not mean for my presence to distress you.'

'No. Yes . . . what I mean is . . . Oh . . . '

'Tell me the whole of it,' he said and smiled. 'Maybe I can help you.'

Jane shook her head. 'No, you cannot help.' Then she changed her mind. 'We are in trouble. Financial trouble.' She hardly dared to look at him. 'I do not know the whole of it except that . . . things are very bad. And . . . ' The last of if came out in a rush. 'I gave two shillings to Leonard Castle. His boat — '

'You hope for a profit?' Daniel interrupted with a voice soft as the sand, yet his words seemed guarded.

'Y-yes,' she confessed.

The waves poured on to the beach and dragged back into the sea in their even rhythm.

'You must go to Mr Castle and ask

for your money back. You must. And you must go quickly. Tomorrow?'

'Tomorrow?' She looked at him. Lines deepened on his brow. 'Yes, I see that I must.'

He gave a thin smile.

'Are you saying that Mr Castle cannot be trusted?' Jane asked.

Daniel took a long breath. 'Go and see him tomorrow and perhaps he will take pity on you. If he does not, then that is the forfeit you have paid for your foolishness.' His voice sounded bitter. 'Leave, and do not speak to anyone, ever, about any of this.'

Jane felt a shiver of fear. She had been foolish.

'What's it like . . . being back?' she said to divert the conversation to another subject.

He put his hands in his pockets. 'In many ways it's the same, in other ways, different.' He looked back out towards the sea, his eyes trained on the distant, grey horizon. 'Anyhow, it matters not as I'm only here a short while.'

Jane opened her mouth to speak, but no immediate words came.

'A man has to make his way in the world,' he said.

'Where are you going?' she managed to ask. 'Back to the Navy?'

He gave a laugh. 'No, I've had my fill of His Majesty's Navy. Fourteen years in that service is plenty enough for one man.'

'What will you do?'

He did not answer. His eyes fixed on the sand at her feet.

'Do you mind me asking?' Jane said.

He took a long breath and looked up at her. 'The Navy is like a cocoon, not a pleasant cocoon, but one nevertheless for there are the walls of the ship around you, food to eat, usually, a hammock to sleep in. You have no need of money in that life. Back on the land here there's a pressing need for coin. I've come to see my aunt, see what the old place is like after all this time. But there's employment for me elsewhere, not here.'

Of course it was difficult to make a living from fishing, Jane thought. That's why so many were happy to be employed in the mines.

'So you're leaving Penhaven?' she asked. She imagined him on the stern of a boat, vessel and man at one, pressing ahead into the wind. Not down a mine, his body bent and his shoulders hunched.

'Falmouth,' he said. Not mining then, although he had still not made clear his plans.

'My brother is going to Falmouth,' Jane said. 'He too must find employment.'

He did not elaborate on his own plans. 'What about you? You're not married?'

'No.' Jane frowned. 'But perhaps it is time for me to marry soon.'

'Marry someone who truly loves you,' Daniel said. 'it is not worth shackling yourself to a life of mediocrity or unhappiness.'

'No . . . Of course.' Could he read

her mind? Jane struggled to think how to turn the conversation on to something else. She did not want to think about John Mandrake now. 'If it's not too much to ask perhaps you might see me home?'

'Certainly.'

They walked in silence the short distance back to within sight of Tregarron House.

* * *

Daniel sat bolt upright in bed. He'd been dreaming.

He reached over and pulled back one curtain. The sky was lightening. It was still early, not long after dawn. He lay back down. He would not rise for a few minutes yet.

His dream had been the familiar one. He had been holding the side of the boat, wading through the sea water, pulling her up towards the beach. The water rode up above his knees. He'd not been so tall then at fifteen.

Why did they do it? It had seemed so easy, then. Simple. It had seemed a trade and commerce available to all, a near-respectable trade for a boy nearing adulthood to embark on. There was good coin to be made, better than the alternatives.

His dream had ended as it always did: the moment when the shouting started and he knew in the pit of his stomach he would be caught.

There were no longer any choices. He knew what he had to do.

The following morning, after they had breakfasted, Jane and her sisters sat in the parlour and worked on their lace.

'It is Papa's birthday tomorrow.' Georgie frowned. 'When are we going to find time to rehearse?'

'Later,' Charlotte replied. 'Mama will be vexed if we do not get a good amount of lace done this morning.'

'We never used to have to work on our lace in the mornings, only ever in the afternoons.' Georgie pouted. 'My fingers hurt.'

126

'Jane?' Mama pushed open the parlour door. Her face had a vague look as if her mind was half-elsewhere. In recent days the worry lines on her brow had deepened. Jane felt a sudden sadness for her Mama. For them all.

'Yes, Mama,' she said. She gave a small smile although her heart wasn't in it.

'We have run out of butter. I need it for the pastry. Will you go to Tolgarth's farm?'

'May I go with Jane?' Georgie piped up.

'No,' Charlotte snapped.

'Yes, dear. Rather, no Georgie, it is better we simply spare Jane for the errand. You are needed here.'

In the hallway, out of sight of the others, Mama gave Jane a single penny. 'Mrs Tolgarth may give you a good sized pat for that,' she said. 'If the milk has been plentiful.'

Jane slipped upstairs and carefully put another two shillings in her reticule.

Getting to Tolgarth's farm would

take her through Penhaven and it would be easy enough to stop by the Castles'. Despite what Daniel Locke had said she had decided what she would do. If it turned out her first investment had brought a fair profit she would re-invest it and add another two shillings besides.

It would never be enough to allow her to escape marrying John Mandrake, she knew. But even a few pennies profit might make a difference. At least Mama would not be scrimping about every pat of butter. Jane concentrated on that thought as she knocked on the door of the Castle's cottage.

Mrs Castle opened the door, looked at her and then shut the door again.

Jane felt a small stab of fear. It was swiftly replaced by anger. How dare Mrs Castle shut the door in her face! Jane knocked on the door again.

And again hard.

The door opened.

'Bide that racket!' Mrs Castle shouted at her. 'What do 'ee want?'

'My mon — .'

A hand reached down and pulled her into the house by her arm. Jane nearly tripped over the step. She found herself in the Castles' front room looking straight into the face of Len Castle. He held her upper arm so firmly it hurt. Jane thought he might shake her.

The door was slammed shut behind her.

She'd never been so close to him before. His face was tanned and pinched like so many of the fishermen, but an ugly scar ran though his left eyebrow cutting it into two jagged pieces.

'The lass has made a mistake.' Mrs Castle's voice was crisp. 'Let 'er go, Len. She doesn't want nothing with you.'

Jane trembled. She had made a mistake. She should never have come here. Not in the first place and not now.

'She's the lass what's to marry Mandrake, Len,' Mrs Castle continued. Jane could hear a sense of urgency in her voice. Somehow, Mrs Castle knew who she was.

'Aye?'

At last his wife seemed to have caught Len Castle's attention. Jane felt the grip on her arm loosen.

'I'm sorry, I have made a mistake,' Jane muttered.

Len Castle grunted, gave her a cruel look and left the room.

Mrs Castle drew back the bolts and opened the door.

Jane ran out of the cottage. Around the corner she slowed to a fast walk and gasped for breath. Her heart pounded in her head. Butter . . . She needed to go to Tolgarth's farm. And after that . . . ?

8

Jane pounded on the door of Mrs Locke's cottage. Her fist hit against the painted wood thrice, no, four times. It hurt. She cradled her hand against her only a moment before trying again.

The door opened.

'Mrs Locke . . . ' Jane could not meet the lady's eyes. She drew in a deep breath. 'Is your nephew — '

'Our Daniel's not here. Gone to Falmouth.'

Not here? The wind whistled past the rocks. A west wind often did so here creating eerie sounds that seemed like voices from another world.

'Jane, you look as pale as a sheet.'

'It is only the cold weather.' Yes, the cold had penetrated through to her bones.

'He'll be back in a day or two, I'll warrant,' Mrs Locke added. 'Will you leave the message with me? Come in. I have the kettle on and the fire is strong.'

'I cannot today. I am sorry.' Jane's mind was racing. Daniel was not here. He was in Falmouth and perhaps not due back for some days. What was she going to do? 'Thank you though. You said he's in Falmouth?'

'Aye, he's some business there. I'll tell him you came by.'

'Th- thank you.' Jane stumbled away. Her head was spinning. She'd thought she would turn to Daniel. It was too far to get to Falmouth, even if she could think of a way of getting there or getting a message there. And Thom was also in Falmouth with Papa, or perhaps she could have turned to him.

She wandered down the path in the direction of the town, not really thinking where she was going. It was no use to speak to Charlotte or Mama of any of this. They would simply be frightened and counsel her to have nothing more to do with any of it.

Yet she could not go and face them tonight alone. What was she to do?

She stopped where she was on the path. Of course, there was always John Mandrake. John Mandrake who, after all, was set to be her husband. Perhaps he would help her? Would he? Or would he be shocked by the whole thing?

One thing was for certain. She could not go and call on John Mandrake, a young gentlewoman alone. She needed Charlotte to come with her for respectability's sake.

Jane made her way back home. Charlotte was alone in the parlour, her lace cushion lain down beside her as she stared out of the front window.

'I saw you come back,' Charlotte said. 'Where have you been?'

'Oh.' For several ticks of the clock Jane found herself at a loss for words. She pushed a stray strand of hair from her face.

'Go on,' Charlotte said.

'It's all rather . . . difficult.' Jane forced her voice to sound strained. 'Charlotte will you help me. Come with me now to see the Mandrakes. Please.'

* ★ *

Daniel stared at the Custom House window. Freshly painted, yet condensation licked the base of each small pane. Beyond and outside, the bustle of Falmouth harbour.

Inside, they waited. Five men, all of them young and all of them carrying firearms. Four were Revenue men, mused Daniel. And himself, the fifth man? He was a man who had been a smuggler. The enemy. Should he in fact be here at all?

The door opened and into the airy room came Samuel Pellew, Collector of Customs at Falmouth, and his deputy. Peder Koskyns, Comptroller. They were both dressed as befitted their stations: wearing silk stockings and breeches and their coat cuffs trimmed with fine lace. It was no secret that the Collector and Comptroller each drew a salary of several hundred pounds a year.

'Good afternoon, gentlemen,' said Mr Pellew, his voice as crisp as the air.

'To business, Mr Koskyns?'

Peder Koskyns spread the map he was carrying on the wide oak table in the middle of the room. 'They'll be using this small cove here.' He pointed at the map, tracing the coastline with his tanned forefinger. 'It is known as Smith's Cove. It is close to Penhaven, but well concealed from view until you are upon the headland above the cove itself.'

'Hear that, Locke?' Peder cast Daniel a brief glance. He stood upright, back from the map for a moment and stroke his chin.

'Yes, sir.' Daniel pushed his shoulders back so that he too stood taller. Peder Koskyns had been in the custom's service for many years. He was Falmouth born and raised. Yet he held no qualms about hunting down his neighbours, if they thought they would evade duties.

'You're a Penhaven man, aren't you, Mr Locke?' Mr Pellew asked, his tone unusually gentle.

'I am.'

'Tell me about Penhaven.'

Six pairs of eyes looked at Daniel and waited.

'Penhaven's like many a village. There's fishing, only fishing doesn't feed a family.' Daniel shifted his weight from one foot to the other. He had been standing for some time. 'One of the smugglers is a young man, no older than I am. Len Castle is his name, and I'll put down good coin that he's leading the proceedings tonight.'

'But this Castle, he's not the mastermind,' interrupted Peder.

'No . . . He's not. There's someone else, someone bigger behind it.' Daniel looked at all the men watching him carefully, their faces trained to show no emotion. Nor would he, though even thinking of the man cast a red blanket of rage in front of his eyes.

He trained his eyes back in the window. He would not jeopardise this by telling them he knew. Only justice would send this man to the gallows. His testimony alone was worth nothing.

'We don't know who is the real leader of the Penhaven gang,' said Peder. 'Maybe he will reveal himself tonight.'

'He, or perchance she,' one of the men joked.

'Let us pray that we do not have a Moll Cutpurse of the seas to contend with,' said Mr Pellew. 'Only the usual gang of cut-throats to apprehend.'

Peder stifled a cough. 'Women and smuggling are like oil and water. An unstable mix.'

★　★　★

'Miss Tregarron and Miss Charlotte Tregarron, what a pleasure.' Mrs Mandrake displayed no surprise at their unexpected visit. 'You will take tea with me, of course. And I will see if my dear son or daughter are at home.'

Jane sat down with Charlotte in the Mandrakes' parlour. Mrs Mandrake rang a small brass bell before sweeping her skirts up with both hands and sitting down on a chaise opposite them.

A servant appeared. A pale-faced young girl in a drab woollen uniform with a starched white cotton apron.

'Please inform Mister John and Miss Diana that Miss Tregarron and Miss Charlotte Tregarron are here.' Mrs Mandrake's voice was sharp. 'And bring tea.'

The fire flickered as if a gust of chilled air had come down the chimney. Jane held her hands together tightly in her lap and willed herself not to start shivering. Despite the fire she felt cold.

'So lovely of you to come,' Mrs Mandrake said. 'Is Mrs Tregarron in good health?'

'Mama is very well,' Charlotte replied.

'I shall have to call on her soon.'

Please do not, Jane thought. They could not afford to keep a fire lit all day in the parlour now. They had no servants. There would be nobody to serve the tea let alone bake cake which could be cut into dainty slices. Mrs Mandrake would see immediately that something was very amiss.

'And Mr Tregarron?' Mrs Mandrake added.

'Papa is well also,' Jane said.

The door opened without a knock. Jane looked up. In stepped John Mandrake and his sister.

Diana came forward and sat down beside her mother. John Mandrake stood in the doorway. He stared towards the ceiling, and Jane followed his gaze upwards to the ornate white plaster rose at its centre. 'Miss Tregarron,' he said. 'I believe that you wished to see me?'

'Yes.'

Now it came to it, her heart seemed to have sunk into her boots. Would he take her seriously, or would he simply think her foolish? She would have to take the risk. They were betrothed, were they not? He had a duty to listen to her, and to assist her if he could.

He led her into the small library and stood still in front of the fire while she walked to the window and back. She wrung her hands together and wondered if he was watching her now, or whether his gaze remained still elsewhere.

'Dear . . . John . . . ' She turned to face him. All his attention seemed to be on the signet ring he wore on his right hand. Her courage nearly left her. 'We are betrothed, and . . . therefore I come to ask for your assistance in a particular matter.'

'Of course.' He did not say, my dear, nor utter any soft words. He twisted the ring one way and then the other.

'I hardly know how to begin.'

'Begin at the beginning,' he replied.

'It started . . . ' Jane faltered. Even now that she had his complete attention, she did not know whether she wanted to tell him.

She talked. He listened. At last she came to the end of it. He had stopped turning the ring and stroked his chin. He said, 'Extraordinary, and quite unthinkable that you should have endangered your own person so.' His eyes remained dull. 'And quite, quite foolish to have speculated good money in this way.'

'I know that I acted unwisely.' Jane lowered her gaze to the richly-patterned carpet.

'Your money is as good as lost. You might as well have thrown it to the bottom of the ocean yourself. When we are married . . . ' He took a long breath. 'Such an eventuality would never occur.'

Was he angry? Jane looked up at him but his expression gave nothing away. 'What will you do?' she asked.

'Of that I am not yet certain.'

Jane waited for him to continue. His gaze flickered, as if he somehow resented her scrutiny.

The fire crackled as a burning log slipped and fell down in the grate.

'You may leave it with me, Miss Tregarron.'

That was it then? A dismissal? Jane opened her mouth to speak.

'Mama will wonder what has taken us so long,' he said. He moved towards the door. 'Let us return to the withdrawing room.'

Jane felt heat steal up her neck. As if . . . as if they had taken their time alone because they had been kissing. No, he had never kissed her. Unexpected vexation pounded in her chest. Not that she wished that he would kiss her, but they were betrothed. Did he not ever consider her in the way that a man is supposed to regard a wife?

Perhaps he wanted to keep such things until they had firmly crossed the boundaries of wedlock.

'Miss Tregarron?' He forced his features into a smile, or so it seemed. 'Have no further concerns on this matter.' He opened the library door for her.

Jane drank tea and ate the small piece of the plain cake she was served, savouring each mouthful and only half listening to the polite talk which took place between Mrs Mandrake, Diana and Charlotte. She would have eaten a second piece of cake. A third even, if it would have been possible.

She walked back home with Charlotte without conversation, ignoring the burning questions that she knew Charlotte silently asked her. What happened with John Mandrake? Why did you need to see him privately?

He had said she need not concern herself further. Yet had he even listened to her properly? The doubts had begun to form even while she was still speaking to him. Nothing John Mandrake had said or done had given her the confidence that she could trust him to act on the matter.

If only Daniel Locke had not gone to Falmouth! She could have spoken with him freely. He would have shared with her his thoughts. He knew . . . Goodness knows what he knew for he had been a smuggler once.

Now, there was nothing else she could do except go to Smith's Cove tonight herself, and watch what was to take place. If the magistrate needed a witness, she would be that witness.

She would stay hidden behind the rocks at the back of the cove. She would be in no real danger.

Len Castle had made a mistake when he had seen fit to steal her money.

*   *   *

'Finish up that piece of belly, Jane.' Mama dabbed her lips with her napkin. 'Good meat it is.' She might as well have added, you are fortunate to have it on your plate at all.

The pork belly tasted only of salt and fat. The pickled onions did little to mask the rancid flavour and the potatoes tasted old and sour.

Supper had been prepared by Charlotte. Had she taken the potatoes from the nearly empty sack in the larder below the shelves of preserves, Jane speculated. There had been wispy traces of mould on them when she had looked at them yesterday.

Jane had taken potatoes from the sack in the outhouse instead. Goodness knows that there was little enough left in the larder. It had always been plentifully stocked when Mrs Beresford had been with them.

Charlotte might have scrubbed the mould off, but the potatoes could still be bad. She could ask Charlotte later, after supper.

She took a last mouthful of the pork and chewed it quickly. It stuck in her throat. She coughed and pushed her knife and fork together on her plate. They used silver cutlery, pretty with its bead pattern, and real china dishes. Why bother when the food was hardly fit to be eaten?

Jane felt tears prickle behind her eyes. She blinked hard to stop them coming. She looked around the table but everyone looked indifferent and Mama was trying to smile.

'Please excuse me,' Charlotte said. Papa nodded and she rose and began to clear the plates.

'I'll help you.' Jane got up and followed Charlotte into the kitchen.

A dull pain stabbed her stomach. She tried to think of something else, anything else than whether the ache in her middle was hunger or an upset.

Outside the dusk penetrated the sky like a soot cloud. As her hands busied with the dishes, her mind moved to the coming night, to a kind of fear that made her hands and feet feel cold, though her heart beat rapidly with excitement. She nearly dropped one of the precious china plates.

'Careful!' exclaimed Charlotte.

Yes, she needed to be careful tonight. She would simply go down to Smith's Cove to see if the landing happened. She would stay hidden among the rocks at the back of the beach.

Yet later, in their bedroom, Charlotte moved one way, then the other in their bed, pulling the blankets with her. Jane let her. The coldness that touched her own limbs in consequence would help make sure she did not fall asleep herself.

At last she heard the deep breathing of Charlotte asleep. She rose and dressed. She slipped out of the house. A chill hung in the black air.

9

Their horses galloped along the ribbon of flat land following the ridge of the bluff coastline, short-cutting the headlands, curving past a dolman and standing stones erected by ancient Britons in times before the written record began.

Now, well-shod hooves churned up the stubble grass, well-brushed flanks gleamed with exertion. They were dressed for the worst kind of weather, in boots, drab oil-skins and black tri-corn hats, damp assaulting their stiffness. Half a dozen men, darkly clothed and their mounts indeterminable chestnut and grey. Only the whites of their eyes stood out against the falling blanket of the dusk.

They pushed onwards. Towards Penhaven. Waves crashed against the outcrop of rocks known as the Coy

Virgins, below where they stopped. So named for they lured men to destruction. There was no lighthouse here, only the grey of scattered clouds shielding the moon from the encroaching night.

Beyond the Coy Virgins and the next headland, a safer cove to land a boat: Smith's Cove.

Daniel wiped his sleeve across his brow. The ride from Falmouth had been hard.

Yet, strangely, his mind was not thinking about what was to come, but of things that had passed. And in particular of one woman he had found crumpled on the ground, motionless and being soaked by heavy rain. A woman who later came to mean more to him than he ever could have credited.

A woman who was to marry someone else.

'Let us dismount,' said Peder, beside him. The wind snatched his voice from him. Behind his silhouette, mauve clouds moved across the greying sky.

Peder turned his head back towards the rest. He said, louder, 'dismount!'

There was a stone ruin. It resembled a small cottage with four stone walls and a gap where the door would have been. It had no roof. Someone had thought to build a lighthouse here a generation past, perhaps thinking they might reverse their dwindling family fortunes from levying light dues.

They had even started on a dwelling for a lighthouse keeper. But the family who owned this land had been ruined by a series of disasters in their tin mines, so that none would work for them. The tinners were a superstitious lot, believing that the spirits living in the mines had somehow been offended and turned malevolent. They moved on to work in safer mines.

It was the best place to tether their horses. The stone walls provided some shelter. They would be undisturbed: it was unlikely that any would pass this way, certainly at night. And Smith's Cove was only a short way farther on foot.

Daniel patted his mount on the neck and fed her a handful of hay he took from his saddle-bag. She was strong and she would ride him away from here and all the way back to Falmouth tonight if he needed her to. She came from the Coach House Inn a little way out of Falmouth. But it had been worth the extra journey to secure the use of her. Peder had found them all good horses.

Peder motioned to them to gather round and stood on a small tuft of grass facing the sea. 'We know why we are here,' he said. His warm breath formed mist in the air. 'The Penhaven Gang. Their untroubled time has come to an end.'

One of their company, a man named Mason, touched his forehead. Perhaps a superstition. Daniel felt the stocks of his pistols. Both were there, nestled snugly. Waiting.

Peder looked about, into the increasing blackness behind and to the side of him. Daniel knew what he was looking for. And there was no sign that the silence lied to them. Did the others know?

It seemed not. 'What is it?' asked Jonah Shovel, his brow furrowing. He was the tallest of them all, with wide shoulders and a broad chest made for rowing.

Peder did not answer immediately. He gave one more glance backwards. 'We are not alone tonight. The Penhaven Gang must be destroyed and, as we know they will be armed, and that they will fight. Therefore Captain Edward Pellew is coming with a troop of marines.'

'God be with us,' said Jonah Shovel and the man named Mason repeated him.

'Why, if the military are to be here, do we not stay at home?' said Daniel. He half-knew the answer but from the way the men glanced at each other he considered that someone had to ask what they were all thinking.

'You mean why not let there be a

bloodbath?' Peder cast his gaze from man to man in the way that only he was able, and made each man feel that his words were especially for him. 'There is a right to trial, the right of fellow-man to dispense justice with the cold facts in front of him, not in the heat of chaos.'

And you would know, Peder did not say, but Daniel was sure he was thinking it. You who escaped an early demise yourself through your fellow-man's mercy and compassion.

Daniel had no answer. He thought instead, as they waited, about frivolous things, and mostly about a woman named Jane Tregarron who would be fast asleep in her bed right now, while they waited out in the cold.

They heard the sound of the officers' horses first: hoof beats and their harnesses, jangling like small bells.

★　★　★

Jane crept down the cliff path to Smith's Cove. Her heart pounded in

152

her ears. She feared with every step that she would miss her footing, or worse — a light shone in her face and discovery.

She had made it down undetected. She sat on the cold sand behind the rocks at the back at the beach. Here she could not be seen from the sea.

All was quiet. Clouds hid the moon and all was enveloped in darkness. Her heart slowed back to its ordinary motion.

She waited.

She wondered if they would come at all. What if she had misheard what had been said? What if they had changed their plans? Would she end up sitting here until dawn in vain?

She looked across the beach, out to sea. Nothing.

Jane found herself thinking of John Mandrake. Perhaps he had tipped off the authorities. And of Daniel Locke. What was his business in Falmouth? What was he doing now? Sleeping? Or in some tavern, carousing? She could not imagine him carousing.

There was something too certain about him. He was the kind of man to enjoy a drink and congenial company, but not one to be swayed by licentiousness or by fripperies.

A light winked up on the dark cliffside. Jane blinked but the light was real. Relaying a message out to sea that the coast was clear, Jane supposed. Something was happening tonight . . .

They would be using a spout lantern. She'd seen one once when she had been a girl. The lantern was completely enclosed and had a spout fashioned on the front out of which shone the light. The light would be seen perfectly well from out at sea but it would be less likely to be seen from the shore.

She could see the light clearly, and they would be able to see it out at sea. Wherever they were. She stared out to sea but it was a pool of ink, and difficult to see where the sea ended and the sky began. The sounds of the waves were regular and quiet. A calm night.

She waited.

Splish-splash. Splish-splash. Jane thought her ears were teasing her at first. But it was unmistakably the oars of a boat. Or boats.

And then she saw them. Hulks, like phantoms, appeared from the dense grey: two gigs, each rowed by several men. She heard the men jumping out to pull the boats on to the shore. And then, the scraping of footsteps upon wet sand, whispered voices, and the occasional thud as they lifted their cargo out on to the beach.

If only she could see exactly what they were doing. Jane could barely make out the individual figures. And she could not see whether it was boxes they carried, or barrels.

More sounds: footsteps. A gang, half a dozen strong, snaked across the beach towards the boats. With them, four mules. She hadn't seen whether they had come down the cliff path or had been hidden somewhere else. Jane felt her breath stop. Pray that they had not been hidden all along and had seen her!

Ka-whoosh! Ka-whoosh! Pistols?

Ka-whoosh! In the corner of her eye she saw the spark from a pistol's flint, somewhere at the far end of the beach.

The men with the mules began to run towards the boats. The men with the boats started moving with rapidity. There was shouting.

There was a muffled sound of movement behind her. A large, gloved hand seized her chin and smothered her mouth and pulled her backwards. She was unable to cry out. She struggled to breathe through her nose. Her captor grasped her hands and held them behind her back.

'Get up!' he shouted gruffly.

Jane stumbled to her feet.

'You're a woman!' He seemed to let his grip slacken around her somewhat, though he kept his hand firmly over her mouth. 'No wonder you've been such a poor look out!' He laughed. 'Didn't see us coming, did you? We saw you though, coming down the cliff path and hiding here.'

I'm not a smuggler, Jane wanted to shout. She struggled but the man's hold around her tightened.

'Calm down, little one.' He lowered his voice. It sounded like a growl. 'You and me are going to wait here quietly and watch it all play out.'

Jane turned her eyes to the middle of the beach where most of the shouting was coming from. She could make out the shapes of men fighting hand to hand and hear the clink of cutlasses. A small breeze moved the clouds and unveiled the moon. Down from the cliff came a swarm of men in uniform: soldiers. The revenue men must have been lying in wait, and they had the support of the militia. John Mandrake had listened to her after all.

If only the man who held her would let her speak! She tried but it came out like a mumbled groan.

'Hush!' he said. 'Save what you wish to say for the magistrate.'

'Put your hands up!' The shout came

out of nowhere. Her captor turned, dragging her with him. They stood face to face with Len Castle, not ten feet away, his pistol primed and held pointed at them with a steady grip.

'Hands up!' Len Castle snapped. 'You hard of hearing?'

Slowly her captor eased his grasp on her, and lifted his hands above his head. She was free!

Ka-whoosh! With a cry, her captor stumbled back and fell to the ground. Len Castle plunged forward towards her.

He could want nothing with her, could he? Before she had even thought what she was doing Jane ran. She could not run into the fighting and the way to the cliff path was blocked by the advancing soldiers. She ran towards the boats.

She heard Len Castle coming after her. She ran as she had never run before. All she could think was to get to the boats, which seemed empty. If she got past the boats she might be able to make it to one of the caves beyond, and hide.

Jane ran past some crates which had been dropped beside one of the mules. The mule brayed and moved towards her but she was too quick for him.

'Get out of the way, stupid animal,' she heard Len Castle shout.

She ran past the stern of the first boat. The water lapped over the tops of her ankle boots and pulled her feet into the sticky sand. She nearly tripped and held on to the side of the second gig to steady herself.

She didn't have that moment to spare. He grabbed her from behind and pulled her down into the shallow water. Jane screamed.

He let her go. She pulled herself to her knees and stood up. Another man held Len Castle by his neckerchief and threw a heavy punch into the side of his face. Len Castle slumped and the man let him fall back into the sea.

'You traitor!' The man said with real anger in his voice.

Len Castle stumbled slowly to his feet and then charged towards him.

Another well aimed blow and Len Castle lay down again, the foam of the waves frothing around him.

'Did you think I'd forget who betrayed me?' the man said.

A moment passed when Jane had no idea what would happen next. She stood where she had got up, transfixed by what was happening before her, and too afraid to run again lest someone else came after her.

Len Castle coughed and spluttered but remained still where he lay.

'Fourteen years,' the man said at last. 'And all that time I never forgot.' He strode over to Len Castle and tried to pull him to his feet.

Len Castle groaned and fell back again as if the sea was a comfortable bed.

'I never forget either.' Another voice. Another man, farther up the shore, walking towards them. He held a pair of pistols trained on the man who'd fought Len Castle. 'I never forget a betrayal either, Daniel Locke.'

Daniel? His silhouette seemed familiar now she looked again. He was the correct height and build. It was Daniel! She wanted to run to him. She couldn't move, or speak.

'Quite what Miss Tregarron is doing here,' the man with the pistols continued, 'I will deal with in good time. First, Mr Locke, it will give me the greatest pleasure to settle the score by putting a bullet between your eyes.'

As he said her name she recognised his voice. John Mandrake.

'No!' Jane threw herself towards him as he trained the first pistol. She knocked into the arm which held it and the pistol misfired into the air. The kick-back sent his elbow slamming into her cheek. She staggered backwards and managed not to cry out with the pain.

A moment later she'd regained her senses, and Daniel Locke had John Mandrake on the ground and was wrestling for the second pistol.

She lifted her foot and ground it down as hard as she could on to John Mandrake's hand. He cried out and let go of the pistol. She kicked it away under the boat, not daring to touch it.

'Take your hands off me,' shouted John Mandrake. 'You'll answer to — '

'No.' Daniel's voice was like iron. He pulled Mr Mandrake's arms tightly together behind his back and held them there. 'You're the one who'll answer to the magistrate.'

John Mandrake's white eyes turned and stared at Jane. He ceased to struggle so much. 'You . . . ' His lips thinned. His breath appeared to leave him. 'You — '

Daniel's fist slammed into his forehead.

Jane turned away. The sour taste of bile rose in her throat.

'Turn him over,' a gruff-sounding man said.

'This one's a gent as well by the looks of him,' said another man. 'C'mon, let's get him trussed up quick as that one yonder looks like he'll stir any moment.'

'You didn't bash that one out hard enough, Mr Locke.'

'No, I did not,' replied Daniel. 'You deal with those two. I'll deal with the woman.'

She heard his footsteps abrading the sand before she felt the strange quality of his nearness. He spoke very quietly. 'Jane? Jane, come with me. Trust me.' Much louder, he said, 'Come with me, woman. No trouble, now, you hear, and I'll not be rough with you.'

A charade.

She walked with him, in step with him, though she dare not look at him lest she catch his eye. She imagined he must be angry with her for being here, though he did not show it. No place for a woman.

The fighting seemed to be over. A small number of marines encircled a small group of smugglers whom one-by-one they handcuffed. Others stood about in scattered small groups. The marines outnumbered the gang considerably. They would never have had a chance, Jane realised. Len Castle, and John Mandrake.

The man she was supposed to marry.

What would happen now? She would never see her money again. The marriage would not go ahead. The memory of all her family sat at supper came into her mind. The rancid pork belly. Sour potatoes. What was to become of them all?

Daniel led her up to a group of three gentlemen, who stood apart from the rest.

'Mr Pellew, Captain Pellew, Mr Koskyns,' Daniel said in a tone that betrayed nothing. 'May I present this young lady. She is Miss Tregarron and lives a short way from here, at Tregarron House, close to Penhaven.'

All three gentleman raised their hats. 'Miss Tregarron?' said one, 'I was acquainted with your grandfather.'

'By a quite unfortunate turn of events,' continued Daniel, 'which I will not embarrass the lady now by relating, she came to be here. It is of my opinion that she is somewhat overset by events, and therefore I ask your permission to return her immediately to her home.'

'Of course, Mr Locke,' one of the gentleman said. 'We will be here some time yet. Come and report to me as soon as you return.'

'Jane?' he said to her as they walked on. 'Are you cold?'

She had not realised that she was shivering. 'Mayhaps I am.'

'You will be warm, in your own bed, soon enough.'

He might have removed his coat and offered her it, Jane considered. But perhaps he did not want to draw attention to them. He insisted she go first up the cliff path and followed her in silence.

When she reached the top, she could keep quiet no longer. There was no possibility they could be heard now.

'I do not know what you think of me, but know this. I came to find you, to tell you all, but your aunt said you had gone to Falmouth, and would not be back. I only went down to the beach tonight, because there was nothing else I could do.'

She did not tell him she had sought out John Mandrake and told him. 'I thought perhaps I might see something or be a witness. I know I was foolish but Len Castle . . . I was so angry that he took my money.'

'Mr Mandrake has been arrested and he will be tried.'

'Yes.'

'And this does not concern you?' Daniel wore a strange expression on his face: impassive yet his eyes creased as though he was confused at her answer.

'It concerns me insofar that his fortune was supposed to save my family from penury,' Jane explained. 'But in truth, I am glad. I never wanted to be his wife. I shall not marry him now, even were he to be acquitted.'

'Marry me.'

10

Jane turned to face him, unsure if she had heard him correctly. 'Marry me,' he repeated.

'Oh, Daniel, you are such a good man.' Jane felt her chest swell with emotion. She was truly fond of him. 'But you do not need to do this. My brother has employment in Falmouth now. My father will sell our house, and invest the proceeds with caution. We shall not starve.'

'I ask for no other reason that I love you,' he replied and confounded her. He brushed the side of her face with one hand, the leather of his gloves made her skin tingle.

He bent his head closer. His warm breath caressed the cold tip of her nose.

His lips touched hers.

She pulled away, alarmed at the suddenness, the heat, the scent of his manliness. He followed, kissed her lightly. Like a caress from a feather. He murmured her name.

She fell into his embrace, breathed him in: soap, horse and leather. His chin scraped her cheek. He kissed her again. She let her lips part. Nothing she had ever experienced had ever been like this. He tasted sweet, yet salty. And completely male.

It ended too quickly. He placed his lips on her forehead, held her closer to him and muttered something the breeze snatched away so she did not hear it.

'Marry me,' he murmured.

'Yes,' Jane replied.

He kissed her again. Her whole being wanted to sing.

He walked her back towards the house.

'Tomorrow, I will come and see your father,' he said.

Jane found she did not want to leave him, not even for a few hours. She was like a piece of lace that he had picked up and continued, completely altering the pattern. It was not possible to unpick it and go back to how things had been before.

Yet she must creep back into the house, and go to bed as if this night had never happened. She managed to say, 'Goodnight, Daniel,' and half-turn away from him.

'Goodnight, my sweetheart.'

★   ★   ★

Daniel caught up with the man he most wished to speak to as he was about to mount his horse.

'Mr Pellew, sir.' Daniel raised his hat. 'Might I ask your permission to address you alone a moment, sir?'

'Mr Locke?' Mr Pellew looked up and disengaged his foot from the stirrup so that he stood squarely on the ground. 'You have returned. Now? Yes, of course.'

'Thank you, sir.'

Mr Pellew patted his mount on the nose. 'Your verdict, Mr Locke, on tonight?'

'Tonight was everything that I hoped

169

it would be,' Daniel answered. He had had his vengeance on Len Castle and John Mandrake, the men who had betrayed him. By rights, it should now all be over.

But he was not sure what he wished to do now. In the Navy, he had seen the threat to England's shores, first-hand. There was a reason for taxation — it paid for the Navy and the Army, who keep England and her Empire safe. And it was just in its own way, the heaviest tax burden was on imported goods like tobacco and spirits, not on the necessities.

'I will tell you this.' Mr Pellew pulled out a gold snuff box from a pocket and took a pinch of the gentleman's weed. 'It was by no means a unanimous decision to take you on. Were it not for the glowing reports from your service in the Navy, I would not have considered your request myself. There are those who say that a leopard can never change his spots, that poacher cannot become gamekeeper, and they will have wagered on your failure.'

'I trust I have proved otherwise,' Daniel said.

'And now, Mr Locke?' Mr Pellew's countenance was stiff and unyielding. 'There is a position for you here in Falmouth, but the decision must be yours. I'll have no half-hearts.'

Daniel felt his fingernails dig into his palms. He wanted the position, but there were important matters to take into account. 'What is the salary, Mr Pellew, sir?'

'Quite adequate for a single man. If he abstains from any significant vices.'

'And for a married man?'

Mr Pellew looked at him directly. 'We shall look again at the particulars, Mr Locke. But rest assured that the Revenue needs men like you.'

★　★　★

Today . . . ? Today was Papa's birthday. Jane pounded the dough to make bread. She would think only on that and nothing else.

Later, they would perform their play. Georgie was very much looking forward to it. They all had worked hard to prepare the costumes and even Thom had been pressed into taking a minor part.

Sunlight streamed through the window and landed in squares across the kitchen table. She should be glad, Jane thought. There had been so many grey and rainy days of late.

Would he come today? Tomorrow? At all? Had it all been some fantastical dream? Had John Mandrake really been arrested?

'Jane?' Charlotte came into the kitchen. 'There is a young man who came to see Papa, and now he is with Mama in the parlour. And Mama asked me to come and make tea and to find you and ask you to go and see Papa. He is in his study. Jane, do you have a suitor?'

'I had better go and see Papa,' Jane said.

Jane washed her hands, removed her apron and went to Papa's study. She knocked on the door.

'Come in.'

Papa sat in his usual chair by his desk. He was alone. Mama and Daniel must be in the parlour as Charlotte had said. It was Daniel who had come wasn't it? Not John Mandrake. A wave of fear rose up inside her.

'Jane?'

She noticed Papa's expression was grave.

'Sit down,' he said.

'Yes, Papa.'

Papa's study held a second leather-covered chair, only used, she supposed, when he had rare visitors of a business nature.

'Papa, tell me what has happened. I can bear it no longer.'

'I had rather thought you might tell me what has happened.' Papa stroked his chin. 'You have an understanding, no, an engagement to be married with one man. This morning another man comes to see me to ask for my permission to address you?'

Relief washed through her like a cool and refreshing drink on a hot day. John Mandrake was not here. It was Daniel.

'Mr Locke?' she said. There must be no confusion.

'Yes. The same Mr Locke, nephew of Mrs Locke, who was convicted of smuggling.' Papa wore a heavy frown.

'He served his time in the Navy, Papa. Fourteen years. He is — '

'He told me. He is reformed, he says. In fact he intends to become a Revenue man. I am to speak with Mr Pellew, Collector of Customs at Falmouth, for a reference.'

'Papa, you must believe him.'

'I am . . . inclined to believe him, Jane. But that is not all that we must consider. You made promises to the Mandrakes, didn't you?'

Jane could keep it within no longer. She rose to her feet. 'A bargain, my hand and this house in return for . . . what? Money? A house in Falmouth?' She heard her voice rise. 'Do you not know that John Mandrake is the worst of them all! He is a smuggler! He runs the smuggling gang here in Penhaven. That is how the Mandrakes are so fortunate.'

'Jane!'

'Do you not realise that they wanted this house because it is the only house which has sight down to Smith's Cove, the cove the smugglers use now. Why, even Georgie saw the free goods they have stored in the caves there.'

'Jane.' Papa's tone was calm. 'Mr Locke has informed us of what happened last night.'

He turned away from her and to his desk. 'I have to say that I harboured some notion that John Mandrake might be involved in the free trade. But . . . not like this.'

'Yet you would have let me marry him!'

'Jane, we have been through some very difficult times. Do sit down please and I will tell you all of it.'

Papa explained how things had been

left when her grandfather had died. Because the mines were no longer workable he had sold the land and invested the money in the London stock market. This had brought a good income for a few years but after a couple of unfortunate investments, their income had begun to dwindle. To counter this he had moved more money into high risk investments.

Papa wrung his hands together. The final blow had come with the collapse of several high risk stocks, all at once within a week of each other. One or two, they could have weathered but not this. He had taken the decision to sell some further high risk stocks and buy government bonds which were a safer investment and would protect their money longer. But this meant their income would be much reduced.

He had gone to John Mandrake to ask for some advice.

'Therefore John Mandrake knew our true circumstances?' Jane asked.

'Yes, he advised me to better spread

my portfolio, which was good advice. We talked about how the portfolio was performing on a number of occasions and he knew exactly my fears that I might have to sell this house. It seemed a generous gesture when he offered to buy this house for a sum over its market value when he married you.'

'And I supposed you agreed there would be no need to provide me with a dowry?'

Papa looked ashamed. 'That is also true.' He leaned forward. 'Jane, Mr Locke tells me that he holds you in very dear affection and will provide for you. However, I do not suppose that a customs officer draws a large salary. Jane, how will you live?'

'I do not know,' Jane replied. In truth she had not thought ahead as to how her life might be with Daniel, only that she trusted him and that it promised happiness.

'Yet you are disposed to accept Mr Locke's suit, should I give him my permission of course?'

'Yes. Yes, Papa.'

'Let us go then to the parlour and ask Mr Locke.'

'Papa!' Jane seized his hands and kissed them. She ran to the study door and opened it.

Daniel sat opposite her mother in the chair in which Thom usually sat. Tea had been poured. More cups waited ready on the tray. Daniel rose to his feet as they entered the room and greeted her father politely.

'Miss Tregarron,' he said. The formality sounded strange.

'Mr Locke,' she replied and sat down next to Mama.

Papa remained standing. He held his hands behind his back. 'Mr Locke, I have consulted with my daughter, Jane, and she is minded to agree to become your wife.'

Jane watched Daniel as he watched her father. He could not stop a smile forming on his face. Jane felt herself smile.

'However,' her father continued,

'there are the practical circumstances to consider . . . '

'Mr Tregarron? Jane?' Daniel looked from Papa to her. 'I have been giving the matter a great deal of thought myself, and one option presents itself. For while it is true that there is a position for me within the Revenue, I do not think the salary will support a man and his wife. Jane, will you come with me to America?'

'America!' Mama cried out. Her hand flew to her mouth.

'Yes, America, Mrs Tregarron.'

Jane saw how Daniel's expression was serious and sincere. She listened carefully as he explained. 'There is a merchant there, one Galen King,' he said, 'whom I was fortunate to meet in Portugal. I did him a small service, that of taking a letter to his sister in Portsmouth. In return I was offered employment in Portsmouth and I began to learn my way as a man of business.'

'I was there a year before coming back here to Penhaven. Just before I left, Mr King sent an offer to me to work for him in Plymouth, Massachusetts. He had a man there who is leaving to set up on his own and he says I may train to be his replacement.'

'This would seem to be a fine opportunity,' Papa remarked.

'Ja — Miss Tregarron, what do you think?' Daniel's expression looked very serious.

'I will come with you to America,' Jane whispered.

'Dear Jane!' Mama raised her hands in agitation. 'How will we do without you?'

'Yes, Papa, how will you?' Jane asked.

'We will do as we planned,' Papa replied. 'Sell this house and buy a small villa in Falmouth. Invest the spare money for an additional income. Thom may still have to work but we will manage.'

'Why do you not come to America?' Jane looked from one parent to the other. 'Invest the money there.'

'Yes, let us go to America.' Mama

spoke with a strength in her voice that Jane had not heard for a long time.

Papa smiled. It was the first time that Jane had seen him smile in months. 'Yes. And now, let us find something to toast the happy pair, and of course, my birthday!'

'Surprise!' Thom, Charlotte, Harriet and Georgie burst into the room, all in their costumes for the play. 'Happy birthday, Papa!' they chorused.

'What is this?' Papa acted surprised. 'A theatrical troupe?'

Harriet stepped forward and took a bow. 'The Tregarron Theatre Company would like to present The Melodrama of the Princess.'

'Jane, quick!' Charlotte said. 'Go and get changed!'

'You haven't heard the news!' Jane protested.

'Jane is to marry Mr Locke and we are all going to America,' Mama said. 'Now run along Jane and get changed. They are waiting for you.'

'America?' Thom queried first. Jane

saw the sparkle of interest in his eye as she left the room.

'You will stay to watch Papa's special birthday play, won't you, Mr Locke?' she heard Georgie press as she fled up the stairs.

'Of course,' he replied as she reached the bedroom door. 'And do call me Daniel. After all, we are nearly family now.'

THE END

We do hope that you have enjoyed reading this large print book.

Did you know that all of our titles are available for purchase?

We publish a wide range of high quality large print books including:
Romances, Mysteries, Classics
General Fiction
Non Fiction and Westerns

Special interest titles available in large print are:
The Little Oxford Dictionary
Music Book, Song Book
Hymn Book, Service Book

Also available from us courtesy of Oxford University Press:
Young Readers' Dictionary
(large print edition)
Young Readers' Thesaurus
(large print edition)

For further information or a free brochure, please contact us at:
Ulverscroft Large Print Books Ltd.,
The Green, Bradgate Road, Anstey,
Leicester, LE7 7FU, England.
Tel: (00 44) **0116 236 4325**
Fax: (00 44) **0116 234 0205**

NUDGING FATE

Marjorie Santer

After being widowed by a car accident Emma Dane decides to make a new life for herself and her young daughter, Jenny, back in the idyllic Norfolk countryside of her childhood. She finds a post teaching at the local school and although she quickly makes friends, the local vet seems determined to be rude and dismissive every time she sees him. Yet, despite his coldness, she can't seem to get him out of her mind . . .

WITH ALL MY LOVE

Patricia Robins

It's 1962, and Jacqueline is fighting the temptation to ignore moral standards and conventions with her fiancé, Chris. Confused by her conflicting feelings, she accepts the offer of a three-week working holiday in Switzerland. Away from home and the steadying influence of Chris, she finds herself desperately attracted to the handsome Antoine. Jackie, still deeply in love with Chris, holds out against Antoine's charms — but then an unlucky skiing accident undermines her good intentions . . .

LEAP OF FAITH

Valerie Holmes

When Carole falls in love she thinks William feels the same about her, but he's a man of faith. Carole is hesitant about expressing her true feelings to him. Then, when she resolves to tell him, his beautiful exgirlfriend arrives and Carole decides to take time out. However, fate throws her handsome childhood hero Jason into her path. Carole chooses to follow her dreams, not knowing that one small step will lead her to take a leap of faith.